SEX, DRUGS, & FASHION

By the same Author

The Human Spirit – Apartheid's unheralded Heroes

When Stars Align

Winds of Change

By One Vote

SEX, DRUGS, & FASHION

A novel by

Carole Eglash-Kosoff

Valley Village Publishing

www.ValleyVillagePublishing.com

Cover Design and Illustration by: James Kirtley; Concept by Arlene Matza-Jackson

Registered WGA West #1676121
Registered Library of Congress Copyright 1-992378771

For more information contact Valley Village publishing at
info@valleyvillagepublishing.com

Website: www.sexdrugsandfashion-thebook.com

10-Digit ISBN 0-9839601-4-3 (e-book)
13-Digit ISBN: 978-0-9839601-4-0 (e-book)

10-Digit ISBN: 0983960119 (Softback)
13-Digit ISBN: 978-0-9839601-1-9 (Softback)

Printed in the United States of America

one

Charlie

"Puta!" He said the profane word with an anger and vitriol that emanated from deep within his very soul. He knew the word would sting...he wanted it to hurt her. He loved his daughter so much...he had expected so much from her and now, the ultimate failure... she was pregnant.

"Don't say that," his wife shouted. "She is not a puta!"

"She spreads her legs for a man she isn't married to...a man old enough to be her father. That is what a puta does," he responded, his voice cracking with emotion.

"Daddy, I'm so sorry," Lorena Gonzalez cried, tears staining her bronze cheeks. "He said he loved me and I loved him. I've been such a fool. When I told him I was pregnant, he just smiled and offered to pay for an abortion. I explained I was Catholic and that wasn't an option. He just shrugged and walked away, muttering 'your choice.' "

"This is your daughter, Rodrigo. She is not a puta! She made a mistake. She isn't the first young girl to be taken in by a man who showers her with gifts."

Rodrigo Gonzalez and his wife, Rosa, had carried their eight-year old daughter from Monterrey, Mexico more than a decade earlier. There was no work and no future in the tiny dirt farm village where they lived, but California, with its promise of opportunity, was a thousand miles to the north and it cast a beacon that illuminated hopes for many in their country.

Coyotes, men who made their living moving people across the border into the United States, had taken them across the last leg of their journey, into the outskirts of Tijuana. When they demanded extra money to cross the border, Rodrigo sent them away. They made their own way, stealthily into National City, where friends picked them up and drove them along back roads into East Los Angeles.

One month, and a fake Green card later, Rodrigo had a job and they began a new life, learning a dozen new words of English each day. It hadn't been easy. Neither he nor his wife could get Driver's Licenses and if they were caught driving without a license they would face immediate deportation. Rosa stayed in her own neighborhood, caring for Lorena. It was Rodrigo who was at risk every day. He took public transportation whenever possible. Rosa became pregnant with a second child but lost the baby in her fourth month. The doctors told her it wasn't safe for them to try again and so she and Rodrigo lavished even more love on their one beautiful daughter.

"You will go to Monterrey and stay with your abuela until the child is born," Rodrigo said, distraught by the unmistakable tragedy of what was happening to his family. Only two years earlier he and his wife had watched their proud daughter, now a young Americanized woman, graduate from the Fashion Institute with honors in apparel design.

Lorena was so lovely and so talented. He'd never regretted working all those extra days to pay the tuition that was much more than they could afford. This was Lorena Gonzalez, the first one in their family to graduate from a college, a girl with a magical smile and twinkle in her voice when she spoke. It had been a struggle, and until now, he'd never regretted it.

"I don't want to go to Mexico. I hated it that one time you made me visit. I barely speak the language."

"You will go. That is final!"

Rodrigo Gonzalez was the Fabric Manager at Galaxy Designs, a successful women's sportswear company. It was located in a stand-alone building on Hill Street in downtown Los Angeles near dozens of other small fabric and garment companies. Galaxy had two divisions. Star Struck catered to the Missy market...a little more conservative...for someone a little older. Starlet was its bread-and-butter Junior Division...younger, more fashion-forward.

In the six years it had been in business, it had grown every year. The company was owned by Charles Barron, a tall, handsome, dark haired Jewish transplant from New York. Barron had learned how to pick people, designers and sales reps, from his earlier years in New York. That apprenticeship is what helped now make him a successful 'garmento.'

Rodrigo carried his daughter's luggage into the Los Angeles Airport's terminal.   Lorena and Rosa walked tearfully behind him.   He was short but strong and barrel-chested from carrying heavy rolls of fabric.

They stopped at the gate.   There would be no last minute reprieve.   Lorena turned and embraced her father. Their love would survive this tragedy.

"Te amo, niña," Rodrigo whispered.

"And I love you, Daddy."

After watching his daughter board the Mexicana DC-3, and drying his wife's tears, he drove to the factory.   He walked into the front offices of Galaxy, past the Koi pond and the white Macaw that were Barron's treasures, past Barron's secretary, and into the large office that housed the company's owner.

"You can't go in there," Judy Kaffer shouted, rising from behind her desk and trying, unsuccessfully, to block the way.

Barron stood as his Fabric Manager stormed into his office.   He knew Rodrigo as a gentle man, hard-working, and a man who kept impeccable records of yards, dye lots, and end cuts.   Charlie also knew that Lorena was Rodrigo's daughter.

"Rodrigo, I'm glad you're here.   I'd….." Charlie's words were cut short by a right fist smashing against his left cheek and into his nose. The blow drove the larger man to the floor, blood spurting everywhere.   Judy and several others watched from the door, inert, startled by the suddenness of the event.

"Someone call the Police!" Judy reacted as Rodrigo walked past her with the same purposeful stride that had carried him into Barron's office.

"No," Barron shouted. "Fuck him! Let him go. Everyone back to work. Judy, get me some ice to stop this damn bleeding, and then get Paul and Susan in here to go over the line. It needs to be in New York ready to show by Friday. Also call Sonny...tell him I need some 'blow' and I need it now." Paul was the Sales Manager for the Junior Division and Susan was a combination Designer Merchandiser. Sonny was Charlie's current local drug source.

Charles Barron had entered the world screaming. Maybe it was the old world ethnic name his parents condemned him with...Shlomo Baronski. The young immigrant was suckled amidst the teeming masses of New York's eastside ghetto. The Baronskis had escaped from the shetls of the Ukraine, along with millions of others, scrimping and saving every kopek and ruble to pay for their steerage passage across the Atlantic. And, after passing through Ellis Island, knowing only a few words of English, Max and Dora, his parents, settled into a one room fourth floor walk-up.

Shlomo grew up on the streets of a small Jewish enclave that housed thousands of families just like his. It was surrounded by similar blocks of Irish, Germans, and Puerto

Ricans.   Ethnic battle lines were at every street corner. It was Kikes versus Guineas versus Krauts versus Greasers and sometimes Niggers.

You stayed on your own block as much as possible to avoid getting a black eye and having your meager lunch money taken. You played stick ball with your friends and if you were Jewish you attended the obligatory Hebrew school to prepare for your Bar Mitzvah when you turned thirteen.

Because the family needed money to survive, Shlomo's formal education was forced to end at the tenth grade. He had just turned fifteen but he was as tall as friends two and three years older.   The family needed money to survive. The dampness of their small apartment and the lack of heat during the city's cold winter brought on Dora's severe tuberculosis, spending money they didn't have for doctors and medicines. The choices came down to food or Shlomo's Hebrew schooling. It was a difficult decision for his parents, albeit an easy one for the young boy who hated each lesson.

If there was an extra dime at the end of the week, Shlomo and his friends went to the movies and stayed for hours watching war movies and cartoons…westerns and newsreels. It was a strange wonderful world for a young boy who had never known anything but the few blocks around him.

Events were cascading around him.   In 1945 the President died…some type of bomb out of science fiction magazines helped end the war…and newsreels told the story of Jews massacred by the millions.   Hundreds of thousands of soldiers were returning and everyone in the country was optimistic about the future.

Max Baronski was a cutter in New York's huge garment industry, spreading the fabric, layer after layer, on long tables and cutting it into the tiny pieces that would later be sewn into a blouse or a dress. The fetid air would eventually foul his lungs and end his life too early, but for now it meant steady income.

Max got his son a job delivering racks of clothing between the contractors who sewed the garments and the warehouse that would ship them. The young boy's education now came from the city's Seventh Avenue Fashion District.

Charlie worked hard. The streets teemed with people who had an energy that easily passed into the young boy's veins. A few months after he started, Shlomo was crossing 39th street, pushing a rack with more than a hundred blouses, when he was accosted by three Puerto Rican teens who knocked him down, grabbed armfuls of clothing and ran off. When it happened again, a month later, this time by three Black kids, he was able to knock one of the kids down before he was hit from behind.

The young man made sure it would never happen again. He began carrying a large switchblade knife which he brandished whenever he felt people approaching. Now, even pedestrians stayed out of his way.

The tall, savvy teen, now calling himself 'Charlie,' had buried Shlomo's name and origin forever. Standing on his toes he could pretend he was nearly six feet tall. He soon would be. There was a shadow of dark fuzz beginning to form on his cheeks and upper lip. His shoulders were growing wide and muscled, and hair was growing between his legs. Adolescence was treating him well.

But it was his deep brown eyes that stopped you...set beneath strong dark eyebrows, they were eyes that reflected a genuine promise of sensuousness. Charlie developed a swagger and a smile that dazzled...first, the young girls, and then the women. Before he started shaving he got his first 'shtup' on bolts of satin in the warehouse, stacked and ready to cut for a Sak's Fifth Avenue order.

"Hey, Charlie, how about a movie this weekend? Born Yesterday with Judy Holiday is at the Roxy. We could go to my place after. I've got some vodka?" It was Sally, a young office girl who was also the niece of the man who owned the cutting service. Charlie liked to flirt with her and found himself surprised when she snuck him into the warehouse for a 'quick-one.' It was. Seconds after she started to pull down his zipper, he came, embarrassed at his inability to control himself. Sally was upset but he fondled her long enough for him to get hard again. When they returned to work, she smiled at him, and giggled. He had taken her cherry, something male friends told him was special. It wasn't. Sally cried and Charlie was afraid he'd lose his job. That was something he couldn't afford to happen. He was going to need to become more selective.

"I'd love to...I really would but my father may want me to go to Temple with him. I'll let you know. I'd much rather be with you," he smiled. It was a smile that made the lie believable.

By the time Charlie turned eighteen, the first 'advisors' were being sent to Vietnam, the Korean war was over and the country was at peace, enjoying prosperity, new music and exciting new fashions.

Now, tall, handsome, confident and twenty-one, Charlie got a job in a showroom, selling sportswear for a small company called Ariana Designs. They produced cheap knock-offs for the budget market, modifying the features of high fashion so that suburban housewives could feel well-dressed at discount prices.

Ariana was owned by Saul Rubenstein, a greasy shmuck who cut corners everywhere he could...thinner fabric, cheaper zippers...whatever it took. But Saul had an eye for sales people who could dazzle the out-of-town buyers. He suggested Charlie shorten his name. Baronski was Anglicized to 'Barron.' He also convinced his young acolyte to upgrade his wardrobe.

A few months later Rubenstein hired a silky, dark-eyed kid from New Jersey, Billy Duval. Billy walked with a comb in one hand, constantly running it through his carefully styled shiny black hair. The other hand he kept free to better express himself, almost as if his hands and mouth were connected. He walked with a slight bounce...a strut that was supposed to imply that men should step aside and girls would be lucky to have him.

He and Charlie disliked one another from the first moment Saul introduced them in the Ariana showroom. They were two young cocks eyeing one another, their testosterone raging.

Billy grew up in the hard scrub areas of Trenton. His father was a trucker and his mother was busy juggling putting food on the table for Billy and three younger siblings. Every few years his Union, the Teamsters, would go out on strike and the family would have even less to eat. Billy tried working but stealing food from the stalls and peddlers was easier and his mother needed the food too much to ask questions. At least once a month his father would walk in toting a big box...a fringe benefit of taking on loads at the dock. Sometimes it was really useless stuff like the time he had a case of puppy food. Meanwhile his kid brother was running numbers for a local mobster. Billy's only goal was getting out of Trenton, the sooner the better.

"Listen, assholes," Saul Rubenstein said. "Only one of you is going to survive and that one will be the one with the most moxie...the one who can generate the biggest orders. Billy, emulate Charlie. He dressed like shit when I hired him a few months ago, now he has a little class...not a lot, but he's getting there. You need to do the same...and put that fucking comb away and stop moving around when you talk. That's all over the top ego-shit. Be cool...the buyers like 'cool.' And call yourself 'Will' or 'William'...'Billy' sounds like you're still popping acne pimples."

Four to five times a year buyers would travel to New York from department stores and specialty shops around the country to place orders for the next season. It was 'Market Week." Most of these buyers were women...young and pretty, and they possessed something very special...a 'magic' pencil...a pencil that could write orders...orders that would translate to sales, profits and commissions...orders that could mean a great deal of money for Charlie and Billy ...money and a better way of life.

"How about some dinner after work, Debbie?" Charlie asked. This girl had dimples the size of Chicago. She was short, blond, and the Buyer from Dayton-Hudson, a large Midwest department store chain. Debbie was no fool. This wasn't her first trip to New York or the first offer of dinner she'd received. She knew she was pretty enough to attract men. She also knew men appreciated more than her blond hair and her perky tits.

Men like Charlie Barron nearly drooled at the size of the orders she could write if she liked the line...both Charlie's and Ariana's. Charlie had watched with amusement as Billy, now Will, made a play for Debbie, showing her a few items while he made small talk. It was too much for the Midwestern girl and she was about to walk out of the showroom when Charlie stepped in. Will moved aside, clearly upset but smart enough to not let the buyer know. He just smiled, seething underneath.

Dayton-Hudson had good luck with Ariana's fall line...it had sold well...well enough for Debbie to place an order for six or eight styles that appealed to her this upcoming spring season, maybe six dozen of each style in two to three colors across a size range. Charlie would be grateful for that kind of an order...really grateful. Her nipples were getting hard just fantasizing about being with Charlie again. He was young, she realized, but he humped with an energy and style far beyond his years, much more than the other men from Ariana she'd enjoyed in the past.

It's impossible to not enjoy a dinner at Lutece, sitting across from a lovely girl who had just earned him nearly a thousand dollars. Dessert was already planned to be at his apartment in the '80's, a fair distance from Manhattan's posh neighborhoods. Charlie always kept a bottle of chilled champagne in his refrigerator...just in case.

The rent was a lot more than he could afford and he shared the small bachelor flat with Bruce Goslin, another single sales friend. Bruce worked for a lingerie company and Charlie would occasionally wander over to his friend's showroom to watch the skimpily clad models parade their new line of bras and satin pajamas.

Each man agreed to be tastefully absent when the other was entertaining. Charlie got the best of that arrangement by a wide margin. He and Bruce grew up together sharing the rigors of PS16, an old crumbling three story elementary school. Theirs was one of those rare boyhood friendships that transcended ethnic differences.

Bruce's father was English, his mother a German refugee. Bruce was hefty...nearly 180 pounds on a strong frame and having a man the size of a football lineman selling 30 denier hosiery in taupe often brought good natured giggles. Bruce laughed with them. He had a smile punctuated with dimples and a large cleft in his chin. And, most important, now that the war was history, he had products to sell. Nylons were the rage now that they were available.

Debbie's order eventually turned out to be much bigger than she intended. She returned to Dayton-Hudson with her thighs sore and a satisfied smile on her face.

"What do you mean you aren't going to pay me full commission on the Dayton order?" Charlie said, staring down at the cigar-chomping Rubenstein.

"Look, kid, you're doing well. Don't fuck it up. We got a low markup on that order. I don't make full profit...you don't make full commission. Capice?"

"I sell at the prices you give me and I expect full commission...you capice?" Charlie said, storming from the company's offices on 34th Street, walking back through an afternoon of New York rain and slush to the showroom. What a bastard, he thought, brushing shoulders with others hurrying along and ignoring their angry stares.

"You ladies are a little early," he said, entering the Ariana showroom and seeing two young attractive women sitting and chatting, fingering some of the fabric swatches.

"Not to worry, Charlie, the ladies and I are getting on famously," Will said, oozing charm. Charlie took a deep breath and struggled to make a personality adjustment from the anger he'd felt against Saul, and now this guy, moving in on his customer. To Charlie, this guy would always be a greasy kid from New Jersey.

"Hi, Charlie," the girls said in near unison. Betty Hutchinson was the Buyer for Burdine's...Sally Johnson was the Buyer for Jordan Marsh, two successful department store chains spread across the south. Sally was twenty-two and spoke with a southern drawl, extending each syllable, and denying the fact that she was born in Vermont and graduated from Penn State University, several hundred miles from the nearest bowl of grits. Betty was a year older and had nearly graduated from Georgia Tech...'nearly' because most of her classes were conducted while she was horizontal beneath the girth of the school's Ramblin' Wreck football team.

The girls met a year earlier and decided to travel together as 'cousins,' making sure their stores didn't sell the same merchandise. They had become adept at mixing colors and styles and insisting that their store's labels were sewn into each garment. They also found safety in being paired up.

"We thought you forgot us," Betty teased, tossing her coifed red hair off her face as she smiled with a sensuousness that recalled the gymnastics she and Charlie shared the previous season.

"How could I do that?" Charlie said, happy to forget his episode with Rubenstein. "I've been looking forward to your visit all week. Shall we do a little business while it's still early? The line looks really good this year. I think it will excite you," he smiled, a glint in his eyes. "Then I thought we'd all go up to the top of the Waldorf after dinner and listen to Bobby Troup for a little while."

"As long as we don't spend the entire evening 'listening,'" Sally drawled, the implication of her tone none too subtle.

Charlie could find no easy way to exclude Will from their evening. He and Sally had already decided to hook up so now it would be a four-some he couldn't avoid. Betty was discriminating in what styles she liked and was willing to order but Sally opted to write whatever her new best friend, Will, suggested. Later as they took the elevator to the Waldorf's roof restaurant, Will gave him a wink. For this evening, at least, they set aside their competitive juices. For this evening they were just two horny guys on a date.

The next morning both men got to the showroom late, each one certain he'd gotten laid better and written a larger order than the other. Charlie won. And this time...the first time, Charlie wouldn't be getting commissions on the Burdines business. Will, on the other hand, was more than satisfied with the outcome.

Market Week, despite its name, generally lasted two weeks and the late nights, long days, and the need to wear a perpetual smile for visiting buyers ended none too soon. Charlie was exhausted. But he couldn't deny that it was productive. He figured he had enough money coming to take a vacation in the Poconos, or maybe even Florida. He'd also love to get his own place. Sharing an apartment with a male friend wasn't his style.

"Hi, Charlie," the girl at Ariana's switchboard said, stopping her gum chewing long enough to smile.

"Hi, Mary. Is our friend in?"

"He's got someone with him and they've been shut up together now for quite a while," she said just as the door swung open and a huge man, still wearing a fedora and his overcoat, turned in the doorway back toward Saul Rubenstein's office.

"You remember what I told you. You let this shit happen again and your goods will be tied up tighter than your asshole. My boss would prefer that our 'relationship' be more pleasant."

The man turned, tipped his hat to Mary, and departed, ignoring Charlie watching the scene unfold.

"What was that about, Saul?" Charlie asked, walking unannounced into the owner's small office. Saul Rubenstein was sitting, collapsed in his chair, his eyes glazed, his left cheek red, slightly raw.

"Get the fuck out of here, Charlie. I'm busy."

"I'm not leaving. I've got a lot of money due me and I want to know when I'm going to get it."

"Fuck your money...I've got bigger problems than your commissions."

"Who was that guy?" Charlie asked.

"He's part of the bent-nose fraternity. They provide protection I don't need, for money I can't afford. They control all the elevator operators. You don't pay, your goods don't move. Fabric doesn't go in, garments don't get shipped," Rubenstein said, holding a handkerchief to his cheek. "...cost of doing business in New York."

"And...it sounds as if you shorted him the money he was expecting the same way you shorted me my commission on the Dayton Hudson order. I just got angry at you, but this guy sounds as if he'll cut your balls off."

"Get out of here, Barron. You'll get your money when I'm good and God-damned ready."

"That shmuck is going to cheat me again, I just know it." Charlie complained, nursing his drink, sitting with Will Duval, Bruce Goslin and Peter Isaacs, a man he hadn't met before.   Peter was part owner, along with his father and uncle, of an embroidery company in New Jersey. He had reluctantly joined his family In the business when he flunked out of Law School. His only other choice was the Army and since someone could get hurt there, he opted for selling embroideries and lace. It wasn't too bad. He got a chance to travel and meet handsome people.

Peter was in his early twenties and he still hadn't decided whether he preferred to be with men or women. He was equally comfortable with both although he'd certainly never be able to bring a boyfriend home to his parents in Trenton. He wasn't ready to deal with both his parents having instant heart attacks. Bruce was aware of Peter's proclivities and smiled at Peter's confusion when he looked at a handsome man and beautiful woman walking together. Once he'd asked Peter which one he preferred but all his friend could do was smile.

They were sitting on adjoining bar stools at Sammy's Roumanian Steak House on Chrystie Street in lower Manhattan. A lot of men from the fashion district made this their mandatory Friday night watering hole.   The buyers had gone home and the men could now entertain themselves before heading home to wives or steady girlfriends.

Sammy's claim to fame was a long, low-ceilinged bar with lots of noise and kosher pickles and cole slaw served up as snacks. The owner, Mr. Rubin...no one knew his first name so they all called him Mr. Rubin, worked the crowd, strolling through the square one-roomed restaurant and playing Hava Nagila on his violin that always had at least one broken string, and wearing the same burgundy t-shirt with the exact same holes every night!

"You know, Charlie," Will said, "If they screw you out of your commissions, I'm going to get shafted as well."

Charlie just nodded, not particularly happy to have Duval tag along. The guy was like an appendage he couldn't cut out and he really didn't give a shit whether the guy got paid at all.

"So, listen to this story," Peter Isaacs says. "You guys remember Gus...big guy, sells budget dresses. He just got married and left the business. It seems he was traveling across the South...Florida, Georgia and Alabama showing the line. He meets a Negro girl...black as night, in one of the Department Stores in Huntsville, Alabama and they are immediately attracted to one another...but this is the South. Anyway, he gets up enough nerve to invite her to dinner. They get in his car and find some diner that will serve them, not easy to find a place that would serve a black and white couple.

After they enjoy dinner and he's made some small talk, he asks her to come back to his motel. She agrees but there is no way the hotel clerk is going to allow a Negro girl into a white hotel. But Gus, being Gus, gets creative and puts her into one of his garment bags and sneaks her to his room. Her name is Naomi. She got pregnant from that night but Gus didn't care. He was in love. Now I hear they've got married and moved to Oregon. You never know."

They were on their third drink when Charlie was loose enough to open up.

"Rubenstein had a visitor this week...a scary mob guy," Charlie said. "He actually smacked Saul around. At another time I might have cheered him on, but this wasn't funny. These guys really are serious about protection payoffs. He warned Saul to keep the episode private ...something like keeping his lips sealed as tight as a camel's butt in a sandstorm. He had me nervous and the guy never even looked at me. I never thought I'd feel sorry for someone I dislike as much as Saul Rubenstein."

"I found out who the guy was," Will interjected. "His name is Joe Valachi. He's strong arm for the Gambino family. They aren't nice people...and they can shut you down or hurt you bad if you cross them. Usually they do it by hassling the guys that work in the building...plumbing gets stopped up, lights don't work, elevators stop running... that sort of thing. If that doesn't work, they use muscle."

"You guys should leave New York," Isaacs said. "The future is Los Angeles...Southern California...beautiful women...movie stars, sunshine...beautiful women, lots of business opportunities...beautiful women. I'm spending more and more time out there selling embroideries. They eat the stuff up. They're happy to put a schmaltzy lace look on everything. Weekends I lie around the hotel swimming pool ogling all the movie star hopefuls and nursing tall drinks that have a cherry and tiny umbrellas hanging from them. There are so many attractive girls in bathing suits, you'd think they reproduce somewhere nearby...like rabbits."

"I don't know," Charlie said, downing one drink and snapping his fingers at the bartender for another. "I like New York. It's got juice...there's always action. I hear L.A. is pretty lay-back...perpetual siesta time."

"It is. That's why people like you and I can generate lots of business there. It's the future ...the movie studios, perpetual summer, and people moving there in droves. The advertisements for new tract homes are hysterical. Whether they're pushing some development two miles or twenty miles away, they claim everything is only a thirty-five minute drive from downtown Los Angeles. And people gobble up these tract homes. Some folks are just tired of shoveling snow six months every year. And GIs back from the war, have no interest in spending thirty years in the same factory doing the same job as their fathers.

"They've also got lots of cheap labor...illegal Mexicans pouring in over the border and too afraid to complain about wages or working conditions. Some come to work on the farms picking lettuce or strawberries, but the women prefer sitting down at a sewing machine...endless supply. I'm telling you, you've got to see it."

"Why not?" Charlie asked, half to himself.

Rubenstein hadn't made a single move to pay Charlie or Will the commissions he owed them. Charlie called Ariana's accountant asking when he might see some money but the old man who took care of the books was

Saul's uncle and he dodged the question expertly. 'Be patient,' he was told. Meanwhile word on the street was that Ariana might not see another season.

"Take it all, fellows...$5.00 a hangar."

"Hey, buddy, have you got a right to sell these samples? Don't they belong to Ariana?"

"You want them," Charlie said. "Don't ask questions. He owes me commission. This is my way of collecting it."

Two hours later Charlie stood and looked around the near empty showroom. He'd waited until Will was spending the day in New Jersey talking to customers. Charlie had even sold some of the fixtures but he'd gotten what he felt was due him. He put an envelope with his resignation in plain sight on the floor of the showroom. In it was a single piece of stationery with one word written in large letters: "Capice!"

two

Los Angeles

A week later, Charlie boarded a huge TWA Constellation from Idyllwild Airport on Long Island. He was going to see what this Southern California phenomenon was all about. Bruce would have their shared apartment entirely to himself for a while. Charlie had a round trip ticket with an open return. He'd give himself plenty of time to scope out what the Coast was all about...

He took his seat, sat back, lit a cigarette, and relaxed. He'd heard that Rubenstein hired some men to find Charlie and get his money back. It seems the shmuck had used Charlie's creative commission reconciliation to skim on the mob again and those boys were pretty unhappy.

"Can I get you a drink, sir?" A uniformed stewardess asked. Below her cap was a face that the Vargas girls of Esquire would be jealous of. Her hair was brown...well, not really brown. When it caught the light reflecting through the airplane's small windows, highlights found blonde fireflies tucked in the waves that surrounded her face, accenting amazing cheek bones. Charlie was entranced. "Thank you. A vodka-seven, Miss....?

"Royce...Jessica Royce. And, if my information is correct, you are Mr. Barron."

"Your information is flawless," he smiled, "As are you."

She smiled and a musical laugh filled the cabin as she turned. Charlie felt an erection pushing against his pants zipper.

The plane stopped to refuel in St. Louis and the passengers disembarked to stretch their legs, but Charlie and Jessica weren't among them. She had brought him three vodka-sevens as they flew southwest at twenty thousand feet above Pennsylvania and Indiana, each encounter more and more suggestive…their verbal sparring leaving no doubt.

Now, alone and on the ground, the two of them stepped into the rear lavatory and locked the door. Charlie helped Jessica remove her jacket in the cramped quarters while they both struggled to stifle their laughter. It was considerably more difficult for Charlie to remove his pants over his shoes.

"This is crazy," Jessica said.

"I just want to know if this qualifies me for membership in the mile-high club."

"I'll give you special dispensation and we'll pretend we're above the clouds. Does that make you feel better?"

"Can't you tell?"

"Well, all I know is if your penis gets any more erect, it will push out into the galley."

"How about if it makes a stop on the way?" he said, pushing her panties down, her skirt already bunched around her waist, her breathing labored.

Jessica Royce was strictly white bread...Methodist, growing up in the Pacific Palisades, an upper class enclave resting in the hills near the Pacific Ocean, with parents who had emigrated from Philadelphia's Main Line. Her father, Bruce, was a stock broker with Merrill, Lynch, and her mother, Sandy, was a professional social climber.

Actually, neither of her parents was strictly Eastern Main Line, more like a nearby tributary. Their families had joined to exile their offspring to California because Bruce and Sandy had both gotten blind drunk as he had driven his car into a water hydrant after side-swiping several parked cars.

The Philadelphia Inquirer's front page pictures of the incident turned out to be a series of articles on the abuses of college drinking. It was all too much for the Royce's tenuous social reputation and the Pacific Ocean was as far west as the young couple could be sent without drowning them. Bruce's father had pulled strings to get his son a job and the couple's going away wedding present was two tickets, and a stateroom, on the California Limited.

'Find yourself a rich Jew-boy' was the constant advice Jessica's mother had given her on the night of her daughter's Sweet Sixteen party. 'They'll always make a good living and treat you good...and most important, they don't make too many sexual demands.'

Jessica graduated from Palisades High School and was taking courses at Santa Monica City College. She had grown to a svelte 5'8" with long shapely legs from swimming three times a week. It was an outdoor pool and she'd watch the airplanes coming and going as she stretched her arms over her head, her legs kicking at the water, in a perfect backstroke.

"We should become stewardesses," she said to her girlfriend, as the two of them walked along the bluff above the beach on a cloudless spring day.

"I'm game. I have no idea what I'm doing in college anyway."

The girls both applied for jobs with Pan-American Airlines. Pan-Am stewardesses wore the smartest blue uniforms and they flew to such exotic locations but Jessica only spoke one language so she wasn't qualified. She did know a little Spanish...por favór...más...and graciás, but that didn't come close to meeting Pan Am's requirements.

Jessica was relieved when TWA offered her a job, and their uniforms of red with white trim looked good on her anyway. But it was the cute red cap that did it. She was a pretty young woman with a good job and lots of opportunities to meet handsome, well-off men.

Now she needed to find a way to follow her mother's advice. She moved out of her parent's home to a small apartment of her own in Manhattan Beach. It was a popular beach community for pilots and stews, just a stone's throw south of the Los Angeles airport. And, during the summer, the sun, sand, and surf brought out the best looking people.

Pilots were always hitting on her. She never met one who was Jewish, though. These Gentile guys were egotistical, sexually adventurous, and always wanted her to go down on them. It wasn't until she had a tryst with a first-class Jewish passenger that she understood the improvement of being with a man who had been circumcised. That was hot...really hot.

"Time to get back to your seat," Jessica smiled as Charlie rearranged his clothes and she tried to fix her face. Her cheeks had become quite ruddy from the sex.

"You girls at TWA really know the meaning of service," Charlie laughed, kissing Jessica on the cheek.

The rest of the flight was without incident, despite the double bounce on landing in Los Angeles.

"Will I see you again?" Charlie asked as he gathered his coat and briefcase.

"Depends! Where are you staying?"

"I have no idea."

"You are kidding, aren't you?"

"No. I have a couple of appointments Thursday but I thought I could spend the next two days seeing the city."

"You can rent a car down by the baggage carousel," she suggested.

"Small problem! I don't drive."

Jessica broke out laughing. "You don't look hopeless. I wouldn't have taken you for a Midwestern boob."

"I'm from New York City. I never needed a car and I didn't think finding a hotel would be much of a struggle."

"Come with me. I have an apartment near the beach and I'm not due to fly out again until Friday."

"There's that TWA service again. How can I refuse?"

Charlie sat back as Jessica wheeled her Karmann Ghia out of the parking lot and headed east to show him some local highlights before heading to her place. Wow, what weather, he thought. The San Gabriel Mountains were clear against a blue sky. There was the Hollywoodland sign and the Griffith Park Observatory. They all looked close enough to touch.

As the car passed the central part of the city, Charlie began to understand what Peter was talking about. Beautiful people were walking along Wilshire Blvd. A little further they passed a large fountain as they entered someplace called Beverly Hills. Then he began to smell salt air.

He sat back. What a welcome, he thought. Imagine...a beautiful city and an amazing girl who has an apartment, wheels, and an ass to die from.

"Here it is, nothing much, but it works for me and when I'm flying, I just lock it up behind me. When I return it's still here waiting for me. You can have the couch."

"Really...the couch," Charlie smiled. "Has our embryonic relationship dimmed already?"

"Let's pretend it's for the decorum and we'll see how everything goes. Do you have a pair of swim trunks with you?"

"No, never thought to bring any."

"We'll go out and pick you up a pair of snazzy briefs and a loud, obnoxious shirt."

"Can I interest you first in some pleasure uncramped by airplane lavatory walls?   As a way of showing my gratitude, of course."

It was sunset before they climbed out of bed and showered.   Charlie stared out the window at his first Pacific sunset, a red orb bouncing above the horizon and reflected in the white caps that kissed the shore.   His thoughts deepened.   This girl was special...not just someone you shagged for a weekend. This was meant to happen.

The next two days were idyllic. They walked the beach, ate fresh seafood, and downed margaritas with salted rims. They gorged themselves on Mexican food and got up early to watch people body surf and walk their dogs along the beach. They made love and went long periods without saying a word.

"Do you think you can drive my Ghia while I'm gone without getting into an accident?" Jessica laughed as Friday approached.

"Is that an invitation to stay here while you're gone?"

"Yes," she said softly. "I think we both want to see how far this will go."

Charlie nodded and took her in his arms.   She fit perfectly...in so many ways.

In the morning, after a night of intense lovemaking, Jessica leaned over and kissed her new lover on the cheek. 'I'll be back Sunday,' a note stuck to the refrigerator announced.

Los Angeles was certainly turning out to be far different than he'd expected. It was a sprawl...spreading in every direction. He knew New York...he understood how to get from point A to point B...but Los Angeles was a mess, no urban plan, no decent public transportation. And, no one walked. Everyone drove their own car. He discovered freeways and drivers blared their horns at him until he understood you could turn right against a red traffic light.

He got a ticket for driving without a license and two warnings for not looking when he changed lanes, but he kept the Ghia intact, its fenders undamaged. He walked the Wilshire Miracle Mile, drove along the famed Sunset Strip, and shopped the malls from North Hollywood to Torrance.

He walked every floor of the shiny Los Angeles Apparel Mart in the midst of what was considered the center of the city. In New York there were several buildings along Seventh Avenue where companies had their showrooms but here, with fewer manufacturers and fewer buyers, they crowded into one large building.

What he noticed more than anything was that people across the area dressed differently. New York's formality was nowhere to be seen. Fabrics here were lighter and brighter...colors were more vibrant. A 'California look' might sell well around the country.

Across the street from the Mart was the Manufacturer's Bank where Peter had arranged for Charlie to meet Sam Simon, one of their Vice-Presidents and a whiz at funding new apparel start-ups. Sitting next to Simon, when he entered the bank, was a young, well-dressed Latin gentleman.

"Mr. Barron," Sam said, rising from his chair. Sam was a squat man, overweight, but the firmness of his handshake and the steadiness of his eyes made you forget his appearance. This man was not to be underestimated...he was for real.

"Let me introduce you to Mr. Pablo Garcia. He is the eldest son of a family that owns a large apparel manufacturing company in El Salvador. His family has been customers of our bank for many years."

Charlie and Pablo shook hands, each one wary of the other.

This 'gringo' looks a little too flashy...a little too New York'ish. What's he doing here? Pablo wondered.

What the fuck is this all about? Charlie blinked in confusion. I came to meet with Sam Simon, not some 'beaner.' On the other hand, the guy doesn't look like most of the dark skinned men I've seen wandering around the city.

This Pablo is slight, average height, but there is something effeminate about him that makes the hair on my arm prickle. And, another thing, when I shook his hand, he stared directly at me, with a slightly curious grin and he held that gaze a little too long. Probably, it's all in my imagination, Charlie thought.

"You two need to get to know one another. You both want the same thing and your backgrounds complement one another. Pablo, your family knows production and they want to back you financially in a woman's apparel company here in Los Angeles. Charlie, you know the marketplace and what designs sell. Your reputation is that you're brash but hard-working...and you're smart. If you two think you can work with one another, our bank will support you."

Sam Simon looked at both men sitting before him...a New York Jew and a kid from Central America. He felt like a puppeteer but he'd been doing this for more than a decade and he had never been wrong. These two kids...Sam thought of most men younger than him as kids, can make a nice living and the bank can make a nice piece of change as well.

Charlie and Pablo were slightly stunned as this man they'd never met laid out their future. Then they each shook hands with the banker, looked at one another and walked toward the exit, unsure of how they were to proceed. They walked across the street to the Mart and, for the next few hours, the two men sat at a booth in Dale's restaurant and talked, about business, about their experiences, about El Salvador and New York. They drank and ate and drank some more. Pablo was married, Charlie wasn't. They'd both grown up toting rolls of fabric.

The bank was long closed before they parted, shaking hands, satisfied with what they'd learned about one another.   The next morning Charlie and Pablo met for breakfast and began walking the floors of the Mart. Charlie pointed out the design details of what was selling...Pablo explained the versatility of the El Salvador factory and what it did best.   Two mornings later they were waiting for the bank to open and Sam to arrive.

"Good morning," he said, dropping into his chair. "How are the two of you getting along?"

"We're ready," Charlie said. Pablo nodded. They each handed the banker checks for $25,000.00 to start the business rolling.

"Congratulations! I'll get the paperwork started."

Pablo would run production and shipping.   Charlie would run Sales and Finance. Sam had arranged for the bank to extend a $100,000 line of credit. He suggested that they factor, finance their accounts receivable, through Heller Financial.   It would give them the cash flow they would need to build a business. Sam's suggestion was as good as a direct order.   All they had to do now was find a designer, a warehouse, and customers.   The two men nodded, shook hands with Sam Simon and one another. They smiled, a little bewildered.   A partnership wasn't something either of them had anticipated.

"What shall we call the new company?" Pablo asked, realizing they needed a name for their new business.

"Christ if I know," Charlie admitted.   "Let's go have a drink to celebrate and think about it."

The two men stood at the corner of 9th and Los Angeles Streets across from the bank.

"How about calling it L A #9?" Charlie asked.

"Not much sex appeal to that."

"How about Starlet? You know, this town is full of young hopefuls, just as we are. It ties in to being a Hollywood company."

"I get it. Why not? Starlet Fashions! Un buen nombre! I guess we're in business."

Charlie had amassed almost $30,000.00 in savings and in the final commissions he'd gathered from selling out Ariana's showroom. Now he was putting most of it in a new start-up with someone he'd never met before. On a whim he took another $1,000.00 and bought an engagement ring, not even sure what Jessica's reaction would be.

"Charlie, are you sure you want to do this? We haven't known one another very long."

"Long enough! Look, I won't deny that I've been with a lot of women. I like women. I'm a healthy male. But this is different. These are feelings I've never felt. I love you."

"But let's get real. I'm not Jewish and I'm sure your family would prefer that you settle down with a nice Jewish girl. I mean my mother will be thrilled I found a Jewish guy to fall in love with, but she's filled with cockamamie ideas on a lot of things."

"Was the phrase 'you loved me' trapped somewhere in that long diatribe?"

"Yes," she sighed. "I do love you and I haven't yet figured out why. All the time I was flying these past few days you were all I could think about."

"Look, this is an engagement ring. We aren't running off to get married. We'll make sure before we tie the knot. Make sense?" he asked, pulling her close to him and taking her face in his hands.

They kissed passionately, and, wordlessly they walked hand in hand to the bedroom where their lovemaking that night was very special for them both.

The following weekend they drove to Tijuana and got married. They had waited long enough.

three

Starlet Fashions

"We need to hire a designer before we do anything else," Charlie said. "How would you feel about bringing out a girl I know from New York? She's a pretty fair talent. She and I had a thing for a while but it never interfered with her work."

"You've just gotten married and you want to transplant someone you've had sex with three thousand miles away. I think I may have a real nutcase for a partner," Pablo laughed.

"Never mind," Charlie said, moving on. "Peter Isaacs gave me some names...designers he sells embroidery to here in L.A. Let's talk to them.

"Too bad, though...my New York lady did like threesomes."

They rented space on the 3d floor of a building on Broadway near the Orpheum Theater that housed dozens of other small garment companies. It was only a two block walk to the Mart. They needed to be in the center of things. Men were busy putting in racks while other men installed telephones or set desks into the small offices that were left over from the previous tenant...a children's wear manufacturer that failed after six months. The attrition rate in garment start-ups was high. "I hope this isn't an unlucky location," Pablo said seriously. "My family sent me the money for my share of the business but they are very nervous about it and this city is a lot more expensive to live in than San Salvador. Besides my wife and I have one daughter and another on the way. We're going to need to get some business quickly. We're starting really late in the season."

"We find a decent designer, get some samples made and you just sit back…you'll watch a master at work," Charlie said confidently.

Six interviews and another dozen resumes later they narrowed their search down to two girls.   Bunny Saxon was a loud mouth Jewish girl who would be impossible to control but seemed to understand how to design a garment that could be manufactured at a reasonable cost. The other girl was Sammy Townsend…Sammy, short for Samantha. She was blond, young, and perky. She seemed both eager and willing to offer more than apparel design. Charlie was interested…Pablo was wary.

"Are you going to be my mother around here?" Charlie laughed. "I'm really old enough to make appropriate business decisions."

"I'm sure your brain can but your reputation says your pecker can't always tell the difference. Let's just hire the Saxon girl. We can produce her designs at the factory in El Salvador for $2.00 a garment less than we can in Los Angeles and maybe keep under the radar of the local Mafia.

"My sources tell me that Tom and Louis Dragna, and their gangster crowd, are trying to unionize all the garment workers in Southern California. They'd be able to exert the same sort of control they've got in New York. They're also trying to shake down the small garment companies. They're a bad crowd."

"The mobsters pulled the same shit where I was working in New York. I hope they don't get a foothold here. Alright, let's hire Miss Red Headed Saxon. We've got a lot of money resting on what she can do."

Bunny Saxon was a talented journeyman. She'd worked for companies in New York and Los Angeles and had her ass pinched more times than she cared to remember. She was good at selecting fabrics and colors. She did her homework, shopping stores, studying fashion magazines. What she wasn't good at was organizing her personal life and picking men who weren't assholes. Whether work was an escape or whether it was easier would take years of therapy to work out. Meanwhile, putting in twelve-hour days was just fine. Her reputation was on the line.

Charlie delayed his flight three times as he, Bunny, and Pablo struggled to put together a line for the fall. He arrived in New York only two days before Market Week ended, his testiness bringing the first spat between he and Jessica. They said a brusque goodbye at the airport. She was off to Minneapolis. He tried apologizing the night before but his words had fallen flat. His mind was on the pressure he was under. If he didn't get enough orders, Starlet would be dead in the water and all their money would be gone.

Two days later the results were barely adequate. Charlie had used his relationships and his cultivated charm to cajole orders from some smaller retail chains but Starlet still hadn't been approved as a vendor with the larger ones. He had one last chance...Mary Withers from Lord & Taylor and he knew what he needed to do to get an order. Mary was the horniest buyer in the city and decent orders were bartered. So much for fidelity in his marriage...so much for his marriage vows!

Mary was no dummy, this was a no-nonsense game with her and she insisted that it be enjoyed in her playground. She had an apartment in the upper '60's where she 'entertained.' Charlie was happy to accommodate her but their sweaty lovemaking had none of the zest she and Charlie had shared in the past.

He had had a great deal to drink, trying hard to keep his visions of Jessica from popping up. His head was still foggy when he awoke in the morning, one arm hanging down to the floor. His fingers felt something crinkly. His eyes were still half closed but it felt familiar. He picked it up and stared. It was a red condom wrapper that had been hidden beneath the bed skirt.

Mary had been busy. He started to put it back when his hand touched a second condom wrapper. This one was white. He was now wide awake and leaned over, pulled up the skirt, and discovered yellow and blue used wrappers. What the hell was going on?

Mary yawned and stretched as she, too, woke from a deep, after good sex, sleep.

"What're you holding?" she asked.

"Condom wrappers," he said, not knowing whether to laugh or be upset.

"What color?"

"The first one I found was red."

"That's you."

"And yellow?"

"That's Philip. He sells for a small accessory company out of Tacoma."

"And blue?"

She laughed. "Pierre...French imports!"

"And white?"

"Hans...German imports."

"Are there more colors?"

"No, just four. If I need to, I rotate them."

"And does the fact that I'm red have any particular significance?"

"It means you are significant enough to have a color. Are you upset? Were you expecting some sort of fidelity?"

"No, but I didn't think your bedroom had its own turnstile."

"Charlie...Charlie...don't be petulant. We've known one another too long and we both know how this game is played."

Mary knew her evening's playmate was now married but she didn't care...that was his business. She could tell, however, that he had been going through the motions with her, clearly not enjoying it with the same enthusiasm that marked their previous trysts. The banter was gone and she made sure Charlie left before breakfast. The order she wrote up reflected both their history and her disappointment. It was well below the $40,000 he had targeted in his mind.

He decided to join his old roommate, Bruce Goslin, for a couple of well-deserved drinks and dinner before catching a late flight back to Los Angeles.

"Did you hear about your old boss, Saul Rubenstein?"

"No. Does he still have a posse out looking for me?"

"I doubt it. They found his body floating in the East River."

"You're kidding," Charlie blanched, recalling the big guy he'd seen in Saul's office.

"Remember last year's introduction of polyvinyl dresses...shiny plastic shit. It was hot and all the young Hollywood types were hyping it in photos. Stores couldn't place orders fast enough. Well, your old cellmate, Will Duval, convinced Saul to jump on the bandwagon.

"Young Will apparently saw large commission checks floating in front of his eyes. But before the first cuts were ready to ship, the demand for the style imploded and all the retailers raced to cancel their orders. Saul got stuck with nearly 800 dresses he couldn't sell at any price."

No one would touch them at any price. Will just shrugged his shoulders. After all, it wasn't his money. But it used up the last of Saul's already stretched credit line. He was royally screwed. The word got around that he had no more cash and he stiffed the mob guys once too often. Apparently they thought that offing Saul would be a signal to others who might feel like doing the same thing."

"Ouch! That's scary shit. The man was a turd but he taught me a lot about this business. How's his family taking it?"

"He left a wife and two sons. He also left a couple of tearful mistresses and an unspecified amount of cash in a safety deposit box."

"Maybe I should send her a condolence letter."

"Who, the wife or the mistresses? Best to leave it alone. They'd still be upset over your emptying the showroom and selling off the samples," Bruce said, sipping his drink.

"And where did Will Duval end up?"

"Now that's a funny thing. The kid is shrewd. He asked the mob guy, Valachi, if he could meet with his boss. I don't know what went on but the mob put one of their own in to run the business and young Will is now running sales. Ariana lives on."

"I guess our Mr. Duval is a survivor...and clever," Charlie acknowledged, raising his glass in a fake tribute.

"How's the new business?" Bruce asked, happy to change the subject. "Starlet...catchy name!"

"Not as good as we'd hoped. It's tough getting a new company off the ground but I'll be going back with some paper and with luck, we'll build from there. It's a competitive jungle out there. Too many companies...too few decent retailers. A lot will take the goods in and then find a reason to return them if they don't sell."

"And marriage...how is that working out for you? Neither one of us ever thought of you as the marrying type. I was shocked when I got the announcement."

"So was I. It just happened. But Jessica is amazing and I really want it to work but chatting it up with all these hot women buyers and merchandisers at these Market Weeks is making it a real test. I spent last night with Mary Withers and you know what that means. I'd need to be a saint and that's hardly my style. I'll be going home with an exhausted smile and a hung over prick."

Bruce laughed. "So much for marital fidelity."

"Amen," Charlie smiled, hoisting his glass.

Pablo walked over to Charlie's desk, holding a stack of papers in his hand. He didn't look happy.

"I totaled up all the orders and there won't be enough shipping the next few months to carry us to spring," he said. "Some of these quantities aren't even enough to cut. The factory in El Salvador will lose money on this type of production."

"We need to manufacture everything we can," Charlie insisted. "Starlet is a new company and some of these are trial orders. We came in late to New York because some of the samples weren't ready. It isn't anyone's fault; we're still trying to figure out what departments we want to end up in at the big stores.

"My relationships got me most of the orders you're holding, but you're right...we don't have enough money to carry us through. I figure we need another ten thousand dollars each."

"That's close to my figure, as well. We'll also need to cut our draws," Pablo confirmed. "I don't know where you'll get yours but you'll be able to hear my family scream all the way from San Salvador when I ask them for 'más dinero.' Any chance Sam Simon at the bank would lend us enough to tide us over?"

"Not a good idea...it could affect our credit line by making them nervous."

Charlie drove home with mixed emotions. He was eager to see Jessica, apologetic for his New York dalliance, and uncomfortable explaining that he didn't have enough to fund the additional money they needed for the business. If Pablo or his family in El Salvador had to put up all the money, Charlie would be a minority owner...not much more than a glorified employee and it wasn't an option he was willing to accept.

"Smells amazing," Charlie said as he entered the apartment, dropping his suitcase on the floor and following the aroma into the kitchen.

"I hope so," Jessica smiled, holding a wooden cooking spoon as she put her arms around her husband's neck. "Did you miss me?"

"More than you know," he said. "I'm sorry I had to go right to the factory. They needed the orders to begin work."

"Did you bring them back lots of business?" she said, handing Charlie a chilled bottle of Chardonnay to open, before returning to stir the contents of a pot steaming on the stove.

"Not as many as I would have liked. I don't think it was the line...most of the buyers liked it. They used nice words like 'fresh,' and 'different,' but a lot of them had already used most of their open-to-buy dollars before I got to them. That means they couldn't place more orders even if they'd wanted to.

"It's going to be difficult to survive until next season without putting more money into the business. Pablo and I both need to ante up again. You don't happen to have a spare ten thousand hidden in your mattress, do you?"

"No, but I might be able to sell my body for a couple of weeks and get it," she laughed, as she wiggled her hips and began setting the table.

"I'm sure you could...I'd certainly pay that much, but no, I intend to keep you all for myself."

"Seriously? You need that much money?" she asked, setting the spoon down and moving closer to Charlie. It was the first time she'd seen doubt in her husband's eyes.

"Ouch! You were so optimistic."

"I still am. This can be good...this really is good," he said, rephrasing his words, buoying them both with conviction.

"I only have a few thousand in savings and you're welcome to it. We girls don't make that much flying around being cute and serving cocktails but my father might be willing to help."

William Royce looked the part of the Eastern patrician with graying sideburns and fourteen ounce wingtip shoes. Sandy Royce, Jessica's mother, had every hair in place, her nails perfectly manicured, and she walked with the erect posture of a woman still balancing an encyclopedia on her head.

Charlie and Jessica had been invited to a casual Sunday afternoon dinner. The four of them had all been together before, of course, but never in the formalized setting of the Royce home, neatly ensconced on a Pacific Palisades hilltop, where even the landscaping had the good sense to have been properly manicured as well. Local ordinances prohibited weeds from residing in the lush Palisades neighborhoods. The living room looked as if it was transplanted from a photo in Sunset and had never been used. White plush carpeting has been brushed into a pattern that, if stepped on, would have been a 3d class felony.

"Tell me about this money you need, Charlie," William Royce asked after the dishes were cleared and coffee was served in demitasse cups.

"The amount my partner and I need to add is another $10,000.00 each. That will carry us to the next big buying season, which is spring. We have a significant amount of orders for our first season but not enough."

"How do you know you aren't going to be throwing good money after bad?"

"The line is good; I still have all my customer contacts, and best of all, we produce these garments in El Salvador for about $2.00 less than any other company selling into the same market. The girl we've got designing is good. She's got a keen eye for spotting trends. We're selling a relaxed sunny California look into a national market. It's really new and fresh. We've looked at the situation from all angles and we're confident we can grow a profitable business."

"It sounds reasonable, and I'd like to help you but I can't just give you the money. I'm sure you understand. I'll loan you the money at 10% interest and I'll expect it all to be repaid within one year."

William Royce never smiled as he made the pronouncement. There was no inkling of concern for his daughter, and certainly not for his Jewish son-in-law."

Charlie stared at the man while silence hung in the room. Jessica was hurt by her father's callousness. Her eyes darted between the man she loved and the other man she thought she knew. Sandy Royce sat, her face unflinching, as if her make-up would crack if she showed any reaction.

So much for family, Charlie thought. The interest rate he was asking would be usury if it was a bank he was talking to, and paying it all back in one year could be tough. But he wasn't comfortable negotiating with his wife's father and William Royce knew it.

"Thank you, Bill," he swallowed. "That's generous of you."

"I'll expect you to secure the loan with your ownership in the company. That's pretty normal, as you know," Royce responded, insulted by being called 'Bill' by someone he had no use for...a suave kike who had taken advantage of his only daughter and would soon foul his family's bloodline with a mixed-breed child.

Charlie struggled to keep calm. The mother-fucker! It wasn't normal and it certainly wasn't fair. All he could think of was 'in for a penny, in for a pound' as he struggled to re-convince himself that this was a sound investment.

"Absolutely," he said. "Draw it up and I'll sign it."

"We have to go," Jessica said, breaking her silence before her husband swung a blow at her father. She knew her husband's anger was tethered just below the surface. "I have to fly out tomorrow."

"Well, it was wonderful being together, the four of us," Sandy said. "We have to do this more often."

As they left, Sandy whispered to her daughter, "I was right about Jewish men, wasn't I?"

Neither Jessica nor Charlie spoke on their drive home along Pacific Coast Highway but Charlie's anger was palpable and Jessica had no idea what she could say to ease the tension. He was angry and speeding along at eighty miles an hour trying to dissipate his fury.

Jessica had initially gotten the impression that her father approved of her choice for a husband but something now told her that Mr. Royce didn't share Mrs. Royce's conviction that it was a good idea to bring a Jew into the family. It sullied the family tree. Wow, she thought. She had certainly never seen that coming.

It was time to get ready for next season and there was plenty to do. Charlie had to make sure that Starlet was a qualified vendor with all the major stores. Heller Financial could help. As Starlet's factor, they lent a prestige to a new business. But ultimately it would be up to Bunny Saxon.

"What about pastels?" Charlie asked. "I hear that pastels will be in next season."

"No way," Bunny said defiantly. "It's going to be brights and prints...lots of frills and colors. Go see a couple of movies...The Pink Panther...Goldfinger...color, color, and more color."

"Are you sure? That's a lot of risk if you're wrong. Maybe we should consider playing it safer. A big mistake and we're toast," Pablo added.

The three of them were working late into the evening. They had munched on greasy tacos from the stand next door and they were all exhausted. Bunny had purchased sample tops to copy from I. Magnin and Bullock's on Wilshire Blvd. Then she had walked the boutiques along Rodeo Drive.

"These are all from the upstairs departments. Do you see pastels...no, you don't! These styles will hit the departments we're shooting for next season. Besides...I'm pretty sure I convinced a friend to put this blouse on Mary Tyler Moore in an upcoming Dick Van Dyke television show. It'll televise in black and white but I'm hoping we get a credit at the end."

"That's wonderful. And you waited until now to tell us? I'll let all the buyers know," Charlie gushed. "And I thought you were just a pretty face."

Pablo left and Charlie stayed to help Bunny straighten up. No need to rush home. Jessica's schedule was requiring her to layover in Seattle.

"You know that you don't really look Jewish," he said, hanging up several blouses.

"I was adopted," Bunny admitted. "They tell me I look more Irish."

"Ah, yes...a lovely colleen from the old country," he jibed. "How about we turn off the lights and enjoy the narrow comfort of our couch?   It could be the first time that old couch has been used for something other than sitting."

"Charlie, didn't your mother ever tell you never to dip your pen in the company ink well?   I like you but you're married."

"You aren't."

"And you're one of the reasons I'm not.   Save your pecker for your wife or your buyers.   You don't need me."

"Can't blame a man for trying," he smiled.

Bunny laughed as they turned off the lights and locked up.

four
Pregnancy

"I'm pregnant," Jessica announced. "One of your little swimmers apparently reached the goal line."

Charlie stammered a 'that's wonderful' and rushed to embrace his wife but in truth he hadn't planned on becoming a father at this point in life. It was another responsibility he hadn't anticipated and certainly didn't need.

Jessica rattled on...due in March...parents will be thrilled...maybe now Charlie's mother will come to visit...will we have the baby circumcised...we never discussed raising the baby Jewish or Protestant...on and on...I'll have to stop working before year's end.

That final utterance was all that Charlie heard. They'd been living off Jessica's salary ever since Charlie and Pablo had to reduce their draws.

Their idyllic life as newlywed lovers had begun to slowly dissipate with neither of them being aware of it. When Jessica wasn't flying she was chattering about children's clothes and names and furniture and weight gain, none of which generated the vaguest interest in Charlie.

Meanwhile, his singular focus was Starlet. He needed a good season. Was the line right...could Pablo's family produce it...did Bunny even know what she was doing?

What if the buyers didn't like it? It knotted his insides from early morning until bedtime. He'd always been able to turn off work during sex but even that wasn't working right now.

Then he met Andy. Andy was a 'nobody' fabric salesman who always seemed to be hanging around.

"Charlie, you need something to relax," Andy said, spreading a white powder into two thin lines onto a small chrome plate. "Here, take a hit of this."

"Thanks but I don't do drugs," Charlie said, pushing the plate away. He'd seen a lot of his friends indulge and telling himself he didn't need it to make himself feel superior. Now he wasn't so sure.

"This isn't drugs...this is the finest Columbian shit. It is guaranteed to clear your head of all the little problems floating around that you'd rather not think about. Take a small hit. That's it...inhale a little into each nostril," he said as Charlie leaned over the table.

"One time, just to see what all the fuss is all about."

The colors cascaded behind his eye lids and the universe appeared ahead of him, endless. All of a sudden he knew which styles would sell and which wouldn't. It was a revelation and he stared at Andy, smiling back at him.

"Told you so."

Charlie left for New York a few days later. Right or wrong, his new white crutch had him focused and soaring with enthusiasm. For those brief days he and Jessica returned to the ardent passion they'd lost. His pregnant wife had no inkling as to what had brought about the transition but she didn't care. The man she loved was back.

"By the time you return, I will have taken my leave of absence from TWA, so I'll be here, arms wide and belly heaving," she smiled, holding her ever protruding midsection.

New York was at its best, the middle of autumn. The leaves were changing color and there was a briskness in the air. The wind blew through the concrete canyons and people walked at a little faster pace.

Charlie felt at home. He'd taken a room at the Mayflower near Midtown. Bruce offered him a bed at their old apartment but this was it for Charlie. All stops out. He'd fuck a goat if the order was large enough.

He had a line of samples he liked and they were priced right. He'd also brought a little of the white security blanket to keep his head clear. Bunny wanted to come...even Pablo had made noises that he was a partner and should be here as well, but this would be Charlie's show. They would have to be bystanders, understanding that their futures depended on the results of the next two weeks.

"Trust me," he averred. "I won't disappoint you."

This season even Mary Withers was satisfied and she smiled as she tore off Charlie's copy of the order following a night she wouldn't forget for a long time. She'd even indulged in a little of Charlie's 'stash.' It was a binge she had never experienced before...and there were no other condom wrappers under the bed.

"Hello, Charlie."

Charlie turned...he knew that voice. He was just coming out of the 1407 building after a long day selling. It was Will Duval.

Will had changed. The swagger was gone but the arrogance remained. He had filled out and was wearing a camel hair coat that had obviously set him back more than a few dollars.

"Will! Nice to see you. You're looking well."

"Yes. I understand you've gotten married and settled down to California suburbia. What brings you to New York?"

"Still in the rag trade. Rumor mill tells me you are now the smiling face of Ariana Fashions."

"Yes. I guess I should thank you for that little stunt you pulled, emptying out the showroom. Saul's backers didn't take kindly to that. It's a good thing you left town. You could have ended up with the same unfortunate results as Saul. But since it all turned out so well for me, I'm disposed to let sleeping dogs lie."

"That's good of you...it keeps the fleas away. You be well." Charlie nodded and walked away.

Will continued to stare at the retreating figure. Our paths will cross again, Charlie Barron. In my book, we still have matters to square.

"I ran into my old friend Will Duval today. He gets greasier every day."

"You run with scum, it rubs off," Bruce Gossett said. Bruce had picked up Charlie at his hotel. They'd have dinner and Bruce would drop his friend off at the airport for a late flight.

"All Will has to do these days is tell his people he needs a better price or better delivery and his mob friends make sure the contractors or the suppliers cooperate," Bruce said, shaking his head.

"Even a donkey could write business with those advantages. Everyone knows about it…even the retailers. The big stores play ball. A few of their top merchandisers have gotten trapped. Either they're pressured to buy styles they know they can't sell or refusing to buy from Ariana and maybe having to write future orders with a broken arm."

Bunny walked around her office and stared at the walls. Starlet was quiet. Everyone had gone home. She picked up a copy of Harper's and flipped the pages, not really looking at anything. She got herself another Coca Cola. She was addicted to them. She lit up a cigarette, inhaled deeply, and closed her eyes. She needed Charlie to be successful. She needed lots of orders to reaffirm her self-image. It was all she had.

Bunny's personal life was nowhere. She'd been dating a part-time sax player, part-time shrink, and part-time flake. She thought it made sense to not date anyone in the garment business but on the other hand those guys didn't understand that a designer was only as good as her last season. The jury was still out on what she, Charlie, and Pablo had settled on, and Charlie had taken with him to New York. If only she'd had a little more time...but she said that every season. It really doesn't matter, she told herself, but she knew that was a lie. It mattered very much.

Pablo wandered around the shipping area. They had overproduced some styles the previous season and some of them were still hanging, lone sentinels that were reminders of their earlier excessive enthusiasm. Not everything they'd produced had been for orders but they never told the factory in El Salvador. He and Charlie had hoped to get some reorder business to ease their cash struggle a little.

His family wasn't happy with Starlet's results thus far. His wife, Alicia, was about to drop their second child. She was beginning to drive him crazy. She'd met some Mormon neighbors and they were preaching salvation to her. They wanted her to go with them to Latter Day Saints services. It was the only path, they were sure, but Alicia was raised to be a staunch Catholic. She was being pulled in two directions and both were away from her husband. All she would talk about when he got home was God...this God...that God, and sin.

Pablo was spending more and more time away from home and if Charlie wasn't successful, there would be nothing in Los Angeles for him. His marriage was a sham and without Starlet, he wouldn't even have enough money to finish the process of getting himself a permanent Green Card. The idea of being deported and sent back to Central America was frightening. He would kill himself.

Meanwhile, he desperately needed to visit his friend, Enrique, again. Enrique was a young hair stylist from Guatemala he'd met a few months ago at a Hispanic Gay bar. He lived with his mother and two sisters. The girls knew he was gay but his mother refused to acknowledge it. Instead, she lit extra candles every Sunday, hoping God would make her fears disappear.

Pablo was sure Alicia knew about Enrique, how could she not? She never said a word or gave him an accusatory glare. She put up a good front, afraid to admit to herself that her husband was a marecón. Why couldn't all this be easier? Why couldn't he and Enrique have a life? At least he didn't need to skulk around seedy gay bars any more. One night stands had always frightened him. What if he ran into someone he knew from his straight life?

Jessica walked along the boardwalk near the house, there dog, Coco, on a leash. Coco was a frisky brown toy poodle that she and Charlie had seen in a pet shop. She had pestered him so hard that Charlie finally gave in. Even now he had to admit the dog was a fun addition to the family. Dogs and new babies go together, they were sure.

What she wasn't sure of any longer was Charlie. She knew he'd taken to sniffing cocaine. It was a drug she was all too familiar with…it came with male ego…it bolstered their testosterone or some such bullshit. It sure did wonders for their sex life. But somehow it made it all less than real. To have your love drug-induced didn't seem right.

Jessica was beginning to think about God. It was God that had given her this life growing inside her. She would repay him, she promised, as she looked at the lights glowing up the shore line in Santa Monica. It was quiet at night but she knew God was out there, watching over her and their baby. She prayed He was watching over Charlie as well.

"A big improvement in orders, don't you think?" Charlie asked, tired from the trip, but satisfied with the results. His biggest disappointment was that Macy's had passed on the line. Gloria, what's her name…their Merchandising Vice President, had torn up the order Charlie had worked so hard to get from their buyer for the Junior department. Macy's would have been a huge coup but Gloria was a niece or a cousin or something related to the now departed Saul Rubenstein and she wasn't about to give Charlie shit. Fuck her…their loss, Charlie thought in an unconvincing way.

"Nice job. I think the factory will be pleased. Bunny, you, too. We couldn't have made this happen without you."

While the factory on the outskirts of San Salvador began production, Charlie relaxed and spent a few days at home.

But Jessica had changed. The gaiety and sexuality of his wife was replaced by a deep solemnity he found very troubling. She kissed him and smiled a lot but his Jessica was gone. Maybe it's the pregnancy, he hoped. Maybe once the baby is born she'll be back. I wonder if she'll ever fly again. How far they'd come since that first hoorah on the TWA plane.

Charlie's life had been a roller coaster since he'd left New York and he was ready for some stability. Starlet wasn't profitable but it wasn't bleeding either. He and Jessica could make it, even if she didn't work. Another year...just give me another year, he thought...a profitable business, a beautiful wife, and a son or daughter. Christ, it all sounded so mature and middle class. It was something he'd never envisioned.

The next season passed without incident, or so it seemed. Charlie spent as much time with Jessica as he could while Pablo balanced his life, uncomfortably, between Alicia and Enrique. The line checked well in most of the stores. Then everything seemed to explode at once.

Twenty-eight hundred miles to the South and twenty kilometers from the outskirts of San Salvador, the followers of Augustin Farabundo Marti and his Central American Socialist Party were stirring up the peasants again. La Matanza, the 1932 Massacre had killed more than twenty thousand of the country's campesinos, had solved nothing.

El Salvador was still controlled by a few rich families and the family of Pablo Garcia was one of them. The discontent of the past still existed. The rebels called strikes, broke machines, and threatened those who worked in the factories. The result was chaos and for Starlet, finished garments they were expecting, arrived damaged, late, or frequently, not at all.

"Now," screamed Jessica. "Oh, my God, I'm dying."

"Hang on. We've timed it. It's only twelve minutes to Torrance Memorial Hospital...I'll get you there in ten," Charlie said, jumping from bed and putting on his pants in a single motion.

Ten minutes and several broken traffic laws later, Jessica was admitted. Charlie let go of her hand as she was wheeled into the Obstetrics Ward. He paced the waiting room with two other impatient men, both smoking one cigarette after another. He went into the Men's room, made sure he was alone, and took out a small case. He arranged a line on his hand and inhaled the white dust. Then he repeated it for the other nostril before washing his hands and looking at himself in the mirror. He managed a deep, relaxing, breath for the first time in hours.

I need my old Jessica back, he said to himself, bent over and holding his head in his hands. Other men had described the nervousness of waiting to become a father, the feeling of utter uselessness. For him, it was more. It was fear...the fear that something bad might happen. Not this time ...please...not this time. His plea was ignored.

The baby was breech and the umbilical cord was caught around the baby's throat. It was too late. The baby was dead. The son Charlie had hoped for was not to be. When he was allowed to see Jessica, her eyes were still damp with tears.

"Charlie, we lost him. We lost our son. I'm so sorry. I wanted this for us."

Charlie dried her tears and kissed her on the forehead. They sat quietly together holding hands as Jessica drifted in and out of sleep, her body quivering with a sorrow only a mother can feel after carrying her baby to term. There wouldn't be another pregnancy. The future that had seemed so certain for he and Jessica had disappeared. He didn't know how he knew it but the love that had brought them together had morphed into something unfamiliar. They would always be friends and he would always care for her but sometime in the near future they would seek their own paths in life.

"What do you mean we're going to lose a third of our orders?" Charlie shouted at his frightened partner.

"The gunmen came into the factory and forced everyone to leave. Outside the building three of the factory supervisors were shot and thrown into a ditch. One of them was my cousin. My brother was wounded and is in the hospital. There is a bullet lodged very close to his heart and they aren't sure they can remove it safely. The workers are all hiding in their homes, afraid to return.

"We always treated our workers well. My father is trying to explain that to the rebels...without the factory, a lot of people won't be able to earn money to feed their families but no one has any idea when they can start producing again."

"Fuck! I'm sorry for your brother but this is our life. We're going to have to get some of these garments made here in L.A."

"They won't look as good and they'll cost us more."

"Some profit is better than none. If we don't ship our orders this season, the stores won't take a chance on us next season. See if Bunny can help you find some local sewing contractors."

Charlie needed another hit...something to stem this onslaught of shit attacking him from every angle. He didn't think that he deserved all these problems and on top of everything he needed to find the $10,000.00 to repay Jessica's father, more, including the interest. He was so sure he'd have the money but now everything was fucked.

"You want to borrow ten large for six months? Have I got that right?"

Charlie had agreed to meet Hefty, no last name, at a seedy restaurant in China Town, just off North Broadway. Hefty was recommended by Andy, Charlie's trusted source for 'blow.' Andy knew someone who knew someone who made hard money loans, no questions asked. It was expensive money but his father-in-law wouldn't hesitate to take his balls, if he could, and dance on them. William Royce had to be repaid and out of his life.

"That's right," Charlie nodded, uncomfortable with both this bull of a man sitting across from him and the smells of rancid cooking oil filling the air from the nearby kitchen.

"Sign here. One year."

"Is there much of a penalty if I'm a little late?"

The man leaned his head back and laughed. "You don't want to be late."

"Jessica, you need to get out of bed and think about reconnecting with TWA. You were happy flying and it gave you purpose. Your life isn't over. Please...we can face tomorrow together."

"Leave me alone. Go back to your disgusting snorting and the buyers you like to fuck."

"Honey," Charlie said, shocked at her outburst. This isn't the woman he'd married.

"We can't bring back the baby. Please, let's not let this destroy us. We can still have a good marriage. We love one another," he pleaded, trying to convince himself as well as Jessica.

"It's God's way of punishing us. Come to the church with me, Charlie...pray with me. Maybe if we both admit to being sinners we can still be saved. Oh, come with me," she urged, reaching out to him as she kneeled on the bed, her arms outstretched.

"Jessica, I'll go to counseling with you if you think it will help but asking for guidance from some mystical being you think is watching our every move is impossible for me.

Think about it...think hard.   Our marriage may depend on it."

Charlie grabbed his jacket and left the apartment.   Coco whined at the door for a few minutes before scampering back onto the bed.

"Oh, Coco, we are all damned.   I can't stay here any longer."

Bhagwan Shree Rajneesh was an Indian mystic with a retreat deep in the hidden crevices of Topanga Canyon, an insulated community of dropouts and those who believed in communal living.   Jessica had visited the Bhagwan's ashram on several occasions and now she chose to disappear into their bosom.   She left a short note, hurriedly scribbled, on their bed. 'I will always love you but I must go. 'May Krishna be with you.'

She didn't tell Charlie where she had gone, nor did she tell any or her friends or her parents.   She had filled one small suitcase, grabbed the dog, and driven off in her Ghia.

"Where is Jessica, Charlie?" Sandy said on the phone, reaching her son-in-law at the factory several days later. Neither she nor her husband had come to the hospital nor reached out to console their daughter over the loss of the baby.   This would have been their first grandchild but it didn't seem to matter to them.

"I'm not really sure.   She left a note saying she'd be gone for a while. I think she's still suffering the loss of our baby. Obviously she hasn't said anything about where she was going to you guys either."

"Well, if you hear from her please let me know. Just a minute, Charlie, William wants to speak with you."

"Charlie," his father-in-law said. "It's that time."

"Bill," he said, hoping to irritate his father-in-law, do you even give a shit that your daughter and I just lost a child and now she's disappeared?"

"Yes, I care...now what about the $11,000.00 that's due? You wouldn't try to 'Jew' me down would you?"

"You are a cold bastard and an insulting bigot. I've got your fucking money. Send over a messenger with a release and I'll give it to him."

"Not necessary. I'll drive down. I've always wanted to see what a Jewish garment business looked like."

Charlie slammed down the receiver and took several deep breaths. How could someone as lovely as Jessica have come from such a warped seed?

Charlie left the money and instructions with the receptionist. Across the envelope he had scrawled 'Fuck You' in large letters. He had no desire to see William Royce. With Jessica not around to restrain him, he wasn't sure he could keep from decking the asshole.

"I won't be back the rest of the day," he said.

The apartment in Manhattan Beach was empty and devoid of all the pleasant memories they'd initially shared.

Jessica and Coco were both gone, nowhere to be found. He hated the silence as he walked the few rooms and the air that reeked with the scent of his failed marriage. He turned on all the lights and fixed himself a drink. At least his father-in-law was out of his life. Damn...where was Jessica, he wondered. An hour later he re-read her note...may Krishna be with you. What the fuck did that mean?

The Ghia was gone. When they needed a second car Charlie had bought himself a Buick but when they were together he preferred the kinkiness of the small Ghia. It was like a first love...it was where he had learned to drive. Now the friendly, responsive little German car was gone and so was his wife. Presumably they were together...but where? He didn't want to be alone but he wasn't sure who he could call. It was past ten when his loneliness got to be too much. He pulled out the little black book he had never told Jessica about and selected a usually available girl.

"Wanda? Charlie here," he shouted a little too loudly into the phone. "What're you doing? No, it's not late. How about I come over? Oh! Then meet me at the Lighthouse in Hermosa Beach. We'll have a late drink and listen to some jazz. Don't say no. I feel like shit and I need some company. Sure...I've got some stuff I can bring. Andy always keeps me well stocked."

Pablo had rented a small apartment on the outskirts of Elysian Park near a hilly protrusion north of downtown called Chavez Ravine. He'd never told Alicia about his special nest. He would just call her and say he was working late. Whatever she might have thought, she kept it to herself. Another quick phone call to say he was available and Enrique would meet him there, often getting there early and fixing dinner for the two of them.

It was almost always weeknights and Tuesdays, particularly, were special. They'd enjoy laughing at the antics of Carol Burnett and Garry Moore on their twelve inch Zenith television set, snuggling in one another's arms on the old couch they'd picked up at the Salvation Army. It was always late when they finally separated with a warm kiss. Tears would drift down Pablo's cheeks as he drove home to what had become a loveless marriage.

It was a grey overcast Sunday morning and Pablo was alone in the house. Alicia had taken their daughter to church somewhere nearby. Pablo opted to stay home on the pretext of cleaning up the yard. He wasn't sure whether his wife had gone to their regular Catholic church or wandered with neighbors into some sacrilegious Mormon place but it was easier to be in the house when she wasn't there. She barely spoke to him anymore and the new baby was due any day.

"I want you to move out," Alicia said when she returned. Their daughter had been dropped off to play at a neighbor's. Her breathing was labored. She was at full term.

"I want you to move out," Alicia said when she returned. Their daughter had been dropped off to play at a neighbor's.

"I cannot live with you any longer. I confessed my suspicions to the Priest and he told me what I must do.

You are a sinful man who does evil things of which I can only imagine. In the olden days you would have been stoned. I will write your family and tell them who you are. You have not only shamed me, you have shamed them as well. I will stay with my cousin while you gather your things. Goodbye Pablo. May God have mercy on you."

Alicia hadn't shed a tear nor had she raised her voice but she had damned him for eternity. Pablo's family would never speak to him again. He would become a pariah. He sat in the kitchen, unmoving, while the sun moved overhead and dusk approached. He heard the door slam when his wife left. There were no goodbyes. There was nothing left to say.   He still had Enrique but without money he knew that even his young lover would desert him.

That Sunday evening, as most homes gathered in their living room to watch the Ed Sullivan show, his neighbors were stunned by the sound of a single gunshot. Someone must have called the police.   They found young, handsome, Pablo Garcia, dead of a bullet to his right temple.

Starlet Fashions was evaporating like a wisp of smoke. Pablo was dead, the factory in El Salvador still hadn't been allowed by the rebels to restart production and Charlie's insides were mush. Maybe there was a God and he was really pissed, Charlie thought. He was numb...even the blow couldn't get him through the 'you take my son...you take my wife...and now you take my partner, a nice kid. Three innocents!' he muttered out loud.

"What the fuck do you want?" he shouted before falling to his knees, sobbing, while everyone stood, inert, outside his office, not knowing whether they still had jobs.

Bunny tried to shake him out of his lethargy but he had lost any desire to move forward. He sat at his desk and stared into space. Jessica was still gone and he hadn't been able to find her. He'd reached out to all her friends but they either didn't know or refused to tell him. Her parents didn't know either. Pablo's father had flown to Los Angeles and wanted to know whether Charlie intended to continue with the business. He left again a few days later, still not knowing. At least Alicia never told the elder Garcia the truth about his son. What difference would it make now?

five

Starting Over

"I need your Driver's License, buddy."

Charlie wasn't even sure where he was or how he'd gotten there. He thought he was somewhere between downtown and Santa Monica and it was sometime between late and early.

"What's that white stuff all over your upper lip?" the policeman asked him, flashing a light onto Charlie's face and seeing his red, bloodshot eyes.

"Probably powdered sugar," Charlie giggled.

"Right. You probably just ate a doughnut. Please get out of the car."

"Officer, is this necessary? I'm sure we can work this out. We're both reasonable men."

A few minutes later Charlie found himself handcuffed in the back of a Beverly Hills police car. Out of the window he could see a tow truck lift his Buick off its front wheels and drive away.

Once he was booked, and still in a drugged haze, he called his lawyer, Tom Snyder. Then he slept...a deep sleep, never moving from a fetal position.

"Barron…wake up," a guard shouted.　"Your bail has been posted.

"Good morning, Charlie," Bunny smiled wanly.　She was

standing next to Tom Snyder, both of them looking a great deal better than Charlie.

They walked out together in silence.　Charlie was embarrassed, angry, and hung over.　His eyes were bloodshot and his body ached from sleeping in the cell.　He was beginning to remember what happened the previous evening.　He and Wanda had hit a few spots, done a few lines, and had a little sex before he got into his car to drive home.　What was wrong with that?

"Can I get some coffee?" he asked, his voice barely above a whisper.

Bunny got him home and onto the bed before he simply collapsed, spread-eagled.　Bunny took a Coke from the refrigerator and lit a cigarette.　She slid open the door to the small patio and sat, watching carefree people below on the nearby sand, tossing balls to one another, dousing themselves with suntan lotion and laughing.

There was a great deal of smiling from the array of local sun worshipers.　It seemed so ironic.　Her life, sans the drugs, wasn't much better than the man she secretly loved, lying akimbo on the bed.　He stirred a few times but it was well into the evening before she found him sitting on the side of the bed, bent over and holding his forehead.

"God, my head sounds like a kettle drum. I need an entire bottle of aspirin. How did I get here? The last thing I remember was partying with Wanda."

"I can fill in part of it," Bunny said, handing Charlie three aspirin and a large, steaming cup of coffee. "But swallow these, drink some coffee, and go take a shower."

Charlie grabbed the cup in both his hands, trying to will them to stop shaking. He started crying and jumped as drops of the hot black liquid from the cup fell onto his bare legs.

"Here, let me take that," Bunny said, putting the cup on the nightstand. "You're at the bottom...it's all up from here." She put his head close to her and stroked his hair. She'd always adored his wavy hair.

Slowly, the tremors in Charlie's system ebbed and he looked up. Their eyes met and he pulled her down and they kissed. She didn't resist.

"I need you," he whispered, his voice hoarse.

"I know you do and I think I need you, too. Just this one time, Charlie, and then we move on with our lives. Agreed?"

He smiled and hesitated.

"I'm not kidding, Charlie. I love you, but I want you as a friend. As a lover or a husband you bring nothing but grief. You can find lots of women to love and have sex with but we both need a special friend. Can we be that to one another? Please!"

"Come here. I'll think about it…I really will, but you know I'm terrible at promises."

"You are a complete shit…"

They were her last words as he whirled her onto the bed and laughed for the first time in, he didn't know, how many days. They swallowed one another voraciously, his hunger trying to blank out the mess he'd made of his life. Bunny responded in kind, giving in to the silent passion she'd had since he first interviewed her for the job.

Nearly an hour later they both lay there, spent.

"Now, we both need a shower and something to eat. Tragedy is yesterday. We're going to resurrect Starlet," he said, kissing Bunny on the cheek before throwing himself from the bed and standing.

"Sam, I want to get the company going again. Do you think you and the bank are willing to help?"

"Charlie, I'd like to but after Heller got their money back, the bank was still short $30,000 on our loan. I haven't seen you in nearly six months and now you show up. What do I tell my managers?

"Sam, I'm on the hook for that money…I understand that, and the best way for you to collect is to let me get back in business. Bunny, the designer, is still with me and Pablo's family might be able to function again."

"I don't think they're interested right now. They're still grieving the loss of their son. Conditions in El Salvador are pretty unsettled and, even here in the States, people are getting nervous about whether they'll have to send their kids to Vietnam if America continues to be involved. They aren't spending as much on clothes. Wait awhile...another season or two, and see how it all sorts itself out."

"Sam, you're wrong. Mary Quant's miniskirts and A-line dresses have people excited. This is a good time."

Sam sat quiet for a few moments as Charlie watched him nervously.

"If I can convince my boss you'll sign a note for the $30,000.00 I might know someone who would work with you," he said, finally, as he snapped his fingers and smiled. It was what made Sam so special...he always knew just the right person.

"Who's that?"

"You know him...Neil Pastore."

"Pastore...that hard-nosed bastard...the guy that owns P & A Fabrics. He's not only a prick...he thinks he's holier than the Pope."

"Good," Sam said sarcastically. "He's all of that but he knows the rag trade and how to make money. He's been wanting to manufacture but he hasn't found the right partner. If you're interested I'll set up a meeting."

Charlie shrugged. "What've I got to lose?"

Sam picked up the phone, dialed, spoke a few minutes and hung up. "He'll see you at his factory on Washington Blvd. at 3:00 PM. Try and keep an open mind until then."

There were a few hours to kill before his meeting so he decided to take a walk and clear his head. The Maple Deli was several blocks away and he'd have enough time to enjoy a good corned beef sandwich. The streets in between were congested with small stores and kiosks. The 'Alley' off Santee was becoming a magnet for buyers interested in close outs at cut prices. Store owners from Mexico would come up north and pay cash for blouses, jeans, and whatever. A lot of the goods were imitations of name brands like Gucci, Yves St. Laurent, and Disney. Most buyers didn't care. They'd peel off cash, paying in 'green' and walk away...no questions asked.

Will Duval was sitting in a booth at the Maple Deli with another man when he entered. His old habit of gesturing wildly as he spoke was still with him and as he saw his old nemesis out of the corner of his eye he knocked over a soft drink bottle on the table.

"Charlie...join us. I won't bite. Sit down! Charlie, this is Hefty Sutton. Hefty, this is Charlie Barron, an old friend from New York."

"What brings you to Los Angeles?" Charlie asked, too tired to avoid the man. After all, given everything he'd gone through, there probably wasn't any more shit in the Universe to throw at him. He and Hefty nodded at one another as Charlie slid into the small booth.

"Don't I know you, Hefty? You look familiar," Charlie said. Hefty Sutton's face wasn't something you'd forget. He was balding but there was a deep scar on his left cheek that caught most of your attention.

"Sure! We've seen one another. Last year...your friend, Andy. You needed money and we lent it to you. We got a good laugh after you asked what happened if you was a little late paying it back. That was funny."

"Right. I guess I better make certain I'm not going to be late."

"Heard you lost a baby, Charlie. Tough break," Will said.

"What are you doing here? I thought you were strictly New York."

"My friends asked me to come out and see about opening a business here in L.A. Say," he said, his eyes lighting up. "How about you run the business in L.A.? You need a new business and my friends are great at making it successful. They get cooperation in places you'd never dream of."

"Thanks, Will, but I've got something already lined up. As a matter of fact, I've got to run. I'm late already."

"Aren't you going to eat?" Hefty asked.

"No, I think I've lost my appetite," he said, standing. "Nice to see you, Will." He couldn't get out of the deli quickly enough. Will working with mobsters in New York was one thing but here in Los Angeles...in his mind he saw Saul Rubenstein floating down the East River but it could have been me, not Saul, he thought, as he walked quickly to where he'd parked his car.

"Neil, nice to see you," Charlie said, amiably.

"Charlie, you're looking good. Sorry to hear about the death of your partner...and the violence in El Salvador...you've had more than your share of bad luck."

"True! Life hasn't been running particularly smooth for me recently."

"Sam says you'd like to get Starlet going again. I always liked what you did with that line. I think it can be a winner."

"I'm glad you think so. I feel the same way."

"So, here's what I'm prepared to do. I'll put up all the capital you need to get it going. I want 60% ownership ...you get 40%, but if the sales and profits are there we'll work out a way for it to become 50-50...equal partners."

"Sounds reasonable provided we put in the specifics on how I get to equal ownership," Charlie said, angry that he'd be at Pastores will until he reached parity.

"A few other things. No more snorting shit. No more cocaine...not at the office...not in your home. Your friend Andy is banned from your life."

"I can make that work," Charlie promised, not sure he could really make that happen.

"And the money you owe the bank comes out of your draw on a regular basis. I suspect you'll have to alter your life style for a while."

"You're putting a pole up my ass, Neil. A lot of what you call 'lifestyle' is what gets me business from a lot of the buyers. And, while we're talking about demands, I have a few as well. First, I need an advance of twelve thousand dollars to pay off loan sharks that helped me fund the business. It's a long story but I need them out of my life."

"I'll front it and you can repay it along with the bank debt. Don't worry...I've never screwed anyone in my life."

Charlie had to keep from laughing. Anyone in this business who claims to have never screwed anyone was someone to be watched very carefully.

"Of course," Charlie agreed, now understanding the kind of man he was dealing with.

"You can control the purse strings and the ownership but I make the operating decisions. I pick the line and my team. I set the sell prices..."

"...as long as they meet the mark-ups we agree to," Neil Pastore interrupted.

"As long as they meet the mark-ups," Charlie agreed, extending his hand. "Do we have a deal?"

"Partner...we've got a deal. Now go to work and get Starlet running. I'll call Sam and let him know."

Charlie felt as if he'd been reborn. His debt had been cleansed and he now had renewed enthusiasm and a reason to move forward from his love for Jessica. He hoped she'd find happiness wherever the hell she disappeared to

I have no idea what to do with the Manhattan Beach apartment, he realized. Most of her things were still there. Do I give them away, put them in storage, or send them to her parent's place? And Coco...she took our dog. Damn it...that was our dog, not hers.

And Pablo...homosexual. Now I understand those strange feelings I'd sensed when the two of us first met, he mused. Pablo was scoping me out. But despite whether Pablo was AC or DC, he was a good partner and a good man. I wonder what makes a man gay...not my style. I prefer big tits, a pretty face, and a hairy pussy.

And no blow from now on. That won't be easy. I've gotten so used to needing a buzz to be on top of my game. Who the fuck am I without that star-studded explosion that brings such clarity, he asked himself. He tried to clear the fog from his thoughts. It was a new day and a new opportunity. He'd started with nothing and he could do it again.

"Listen, Sandy," he said to Starlet's receptionist a few days later when he'd been able to contact everyone and get them working again. "You know my friend, Andy...short, balding guy?"

"Yes, the brash guy who thinks he can go where he wants."

"You aren't to let him in here anymore. Whatever it takes...get rid of him."

"I know," she answered without hesitancy.

"How do you know?"

"A Mr. Pastore already called and introduced himself as your new partner. He told me to keep your friend, Andy, out of the place. That's OK, isn't it?"

"Sure...thanks," Charlie said. My new partner isn't going to take any chances, is he?

Neil Pastore had gotten what he wanted. He usually did. He sat back and stroked his mustache.

"Georgia, get me some coffee," he shouted to his secretary. Within minutes a 5'9" mid-30's blond, well-endowed, entered, carrying a steaming cup of coffee resting on a saucer of bone china. She set it down gently on the corner of his desk.

"I like your new partner, Mr. Pastore. He's awfully cute."

"Georgia, his favorite pastime is fucking like a rabbit. If you'd be interested, I'm sure I can arrange something for you. Then I'd be both your boss and your pimp."

"Neil...stop it," she whispered. She only called him Neil when they were alone or when he was being naughty. She knew he loved to shock her. She came around behind him and began to massage his shoulders.

"You're very tense," she said, kneading the nape of his neck.

"You know how to solve that problem," he said matter-of-factly, not turning around, "better than anyone I know."

"Of course I do," she said, turning Neil's chair around, unbuckling his belt, and pulling down his pants zipper.

Pastore adjusted his position. A smug but contented look came across his face. He closed his eyes as Georgia bent down and eased his shorts off. He could feel himself get erect as she slid her fingers gently up and down his soft, white shaft before cupping his sac and taking his penis into her mouth.

"Georgia," he sighed, arching his back and clinching his teeth. "Oh, my God!"

He came as she tried to grab a Kleenex. She hated to have him come in her mouth but the older he got, the less control he had, and it was more and more difficult for her to time the moment.

"Was that good?" she asked, standing and turning aside to wipe her mouth.

"You know it was...it always is," he said, lazily beginning to rearrange his clothes.

She smiled. They'd been together now more than five years. There were no misconceptions about their relationship. She knew he'd never leave his wife and marry her, but he did promise to see that she was taken care of. He was almost old enough to be her father and he'd be insulted if she ever asked him to put that promise in writing.

She'd just have to hope that the future worked out for her. Anything was better than the lousy marriage she had with a neer-do-well who thought he was another Picasso and hadn't sold a painting in recent memory.

Neil Pastore was that odd breed…an Italian Jew. His father had been Mayor of a small Italian town. His mother was from an Orthodox Jewish family originally from Morocco. She was the daughter of a wealthy art collector. When Mussolini came to power and fell under the sway of Adolph Hitler, Jews were rounded up, their property confiscated, and they were herded into camps.

The Pastores escaped, thanks to cousins who had earlier immigrated into Ethiopia. What works of art they could roll up and take with them or convert to cash would be all the wealth they would have. Neil and his sister were young adults when this was taking place, forced to leave their friends and the only life they'd known. They had no desire to remain in the cultural abyss of a small African country. Once their parents were settled, brother and sister said goodbye to their parents and traveled to Venezuela before traversing to New York. A few years later Neil's sister married another Jewish refugee and settled down to become a housewife with a husband and three young children in Scarsdale, a New York suburb.

"Are we still driving to Las Vegas this weekend, Neil?" Georgia asked. She had told her husband she was leaving Friday to visit her sister in Fresno. He didn't care. Weekends she never saw him. He played golf both days and stayed late at his club to get blotto. Screw him…he had his life, she had hers.

"If you'd like, although I'm thinking maybe we should fly. I hate that six to seven hour drive. But, yes, plan on it. We'll leave from work. Would you like some fresh clothes? I want to see how Starlet is doing. You can come with me."

"Hi, you must be Sandy. Call me Neil. You'll probably see a lot of me. This is my secretary, Georgia. Is Charlie in?"

"No, he's at the showroom. Is there anything I can help you with?"

"No, that's OK. We'll just wander around."

"This would look good on you, Georgia," he said, picking a garment off the rack.

"Put that back," Bunny shouted, walking away from the fit model who was trying on a blouse for the coming season.

"Who are you?" Neil frowned.

"I'm Bunny Saxon, and you shouldn't be wandering around here."

"Well, I'm Neil Pastore and I own most of this place so keep your sass for someone else."

"That may entitle you to be here but if you want a line ready for New York you'll leave all these garments alone."

"You're a piece of work, aren't you," he laughed. "But Charlie tells me you have talent. You'll have to finish your line without this top. I've already promised it to Georgia."

"Well, un-promise it," Bunny insisted. "I spent $150 on that top at Sak's. We're knocking it off and it should be one of the better sellers in the line. We copy it...then we return it. Can't your Miss Georgia wait for a copy that comes from Starlet."

"No, she can't, because I don't want her to. I want this one. Now, go back to work, I assume you're busy."

"Thanks for your concern but I need a break." Bunny walked away, her cheeks nearly as red as her hair.

Neil Pastore laughed. "Designers...they're all prima donnas. Here Georgia...Starlet's gift to you. Let's get out of here."

"I'm asking you nicely, Neil. Stay the fuck out of the factory unless I'm there. It's a place of business and we're on a tight schedule. If you want Starlet to succeed, you can't disrupt it. Is that understood?" Charlie said on the phone, trying to keep his cool.

"I hear you, Charlie...I really do. But you can go fuck yourself. I've got a lot of money in that place and I intend to keep an eye on what's going on. Is that understood? Now...you keep working. Georgia and I are going to Vegas for the weekend. Don Rickles is starring at the Desert Inn and we've been comp'd with a poolside cabana. I'll try not to think about you. "

SIX

Ruby

Neil Pastore had built a successful fabric company from scratch. His first job was as a young rep selling denim for Cone Mills. The market for jeans had exploded and neither Levi Strauss nor Lee Jeans were able to produce enough product to keep pace. There was more demand than fabric...the blue cloth was at a premium. Neil used that shortage to make extra money from those apparel companies willing to pay another dime or quarter a yard, on the side, directly to him, to make sure they got priority on delivery.

He then started brokering greige goods...raw unfinished rolls from which companies could dye or print on. Apparel companies across the city loved having a local source. Two years later Neil also introduced cotton acrylic fabric into the market. Each venture...each innovation, brought him more money.

His personal life was different. He dressed like a dandy, often wearing seersucker suits or throwing a cape over his shoulders for effect. He was short, not much more than 5'6" even with the elevated heels on his shoes...and he loved tall, blond women. At home he had a short wife and three daughters, all of whom were enrolled in private schools.

His wife, Rebecca, a plain girl from Yonkers, enjoyed motherhood, and celebrating the Jewish holidays. What she didn't like was sex. Having three children was enough and the weight she gained after birthing each of them never seemed to disappear, no matter how many fad diets she tried. She dyed the roots of her graying brown hair.

She got facials and massages. She shopped continuously. But nothing she did mattered. She had become an old house 'frau.'

Romance between Rebecca and her husband was gone and if Neil wanted to take his pleasures elsewhere, that was alright with her. He just needed to be circumspect. The family were members of a Conservative Jewish Temple in Brentwood. Neil was also a member of the Italian-American Society and one of the first Jews granted membership in the Brentwood Country Club once it had gotten rid of its restrictions.

Phyllis, their eldest daughter, was about to turn thirteen and her parents had planned a huge Bat Mitzvah, a coming of age party meant to celebrate the parent's wealth more than their daughter's achievement. Two hundred of their closest friends were invited to a sit down dinner at the nearby exclusive Beverly Hills Hotel. One of those guests was Charlie Barron.

A few weeks earlier a messenger had come into the offices of Starlet with a large envelope addressed to Charles Barron – Personal. Jessica had served him with divorce papers. Charlie shut his door and called the phone number of her attorney, Roger Nethers.

"Mr. Nethers, this is all a mistake. If you can tell me how to reach Jessica, I'm sure that she and I can work things out."

"I'm sorry, Mr. Barron, I have very specific instructions to keep her whereabouts a secret. Please sign the papers and messenger them back to me. She would prefer that this be kept amicable. She said to tell you if you called that she wished you well but she has found her righteous path in life and she hopes you will let her go."

"And if I don't?" he asked.

"She will be very disappointed. She has no intention of ever remarrying and she isn't seeking alimony but you might want to remarry someday and have children. It's the best thing, Mr. Barron. And, if I may add my own thoughts, there is a serenity about Jessica that one rarely sees. She seems to have found an inner peace. If you love her, do this for her."

His thoughts drifted back to their first encounter on the airplane, the two of them holding hands walking on the beach, buying the dog...and then that terrible day at the hospital. It all flashed by in a second. Charlie got up an poured himself a drink and sat, staring at a picture of he and Jessica that he kept in his desk drawer. They were both laughing and mugging into the camera at an Amusement Park. Charlie cried as he signed the papers. Jessica would now be just a wonderful memory.

Charlie could hear the music from the moment he turned his Buick over to the parking valet at the hotel's roundabout. Handsome, well-turned out people, moved toward the Ballroom. Many of the women were bedecked in mink, despite the evening's balmy weather.

"Champagne, sir?" a waiter asked, carrying a tray of goblets filled with their bubbling nectar.

"Is there an open bar?" Charlie asked.

"Of course. Walk straight through. It will be on your left."

Charlie moved through the milling crowd of near strangers greeting one another like distant family members. Girlfriends had been put aside for the evening. It would be inexcusable to bring someone other than your wife…it would be a 'shanda', a breach of Jewish etiquette.

"Dewar's on the rocks," Charlie asked, elbowing his way to the front of the crowded bar.

"Can you get me an old fashioned?" a soft, feminine voice asked from somewhere behind him, stretching her arm to rest on his shoulder.

He turned and smiled at the cute brunette grinning back at him. She was petite but with a face most artists would describe as aquiline.

"And an old fashioned, bartender."

"Here you are, Miss….?" Charlie said, pushing back from the crowd and staring down into the prettiest face he'd seen since Jessica.

"Ruby Taylor! Thank you for the drink, Mr...."

"Charlie...Charlie Barron. Ruby, what an enchanting name. Are you enchanting, Miss Taylor?"

She laughed...a light, lyrical laugh.

"Nice line...quite novel." It was said with an assurance that excited him.

"Wasn't your husband or date chivalrous enough to get you a drink?"

"I'm sure he would if he was here tonight but he's on location...somewhere in New Mexico, I think. He asked me to make an appearance on his behalf."

"Dangerous to come to this type of event alone," Charlie teased. "You could be attacked by an insane Rabbi. Since I'm here alone as well, can I offer you my protection?"

"Thank you, Mr. Barron, but who will protect me from you?"

"Aha, but I am your gallant Lochinvar, granting your every wish." He guided her to the balcony, away from the guests crowding around platters of shrimp and rumaki, both considered 'traif' in more Orthodox and Conservative celebrations. Neil had decided to flaunt that tradition.

Ruby was wearing a simple black dress, a wide swath of cloth over one shoulder...the other shoulder bare, very Grecian and seductive. The dress was ankle length but cut high in front. Her breasts popped like small melons and Charlie was doing all he could to keep his eyes on her face. It wasn't difficult. Her green eyes had reached out and snapped them to her.

They sat together at a table near the rear of the huge ballroom while the Bat Mitzvah girl thanked her parents, her grandparents, her aunts and uncles and everyone else in Brentwood. Ten minutes into her soliloquy, Charlie took Ruby's hand, looked at her, and they slid out of the room.

He retrieved his car, promising they would return for hers later and he drove off, racing down Sunset Blvd. toward Pacific Coast Highway and the beach. He parked facing the ocean, a huge moon casting its special light and kissing the waves that moved in a steady, never ending procession. Charlie remembered the first time he'd seen a similar sight and a pang of sadness yanked inside him.

"A penny for your thoughts," Ruby said, lighting a cigarette and passing it to him.

"Not worth it," Charlie said, taking the cigarette, tossing it out the window, leaning over and kissing this marvelous girl who had fallen from the sky. His mouth opened and she followed suit, her tongue playing against his, biting his lip lightly as she stroked his cheek.

"You're good at this," he said.

"I haven't been a Girl Scout for several years but I had won several merit badges when I was younger."

"Shall we move into the back seat for more comfort?" Charlie asked.

"I don't think so," she said, not upset, but with a tone that meant 'not tonight.'

"How about a drink at the Miramar?"

"Much better idea."

"Dewar's neat and an old-fashioned," he ordered for them both as they sat close together in a dark corner booth.

"Now, tell me, Ruby Taylor. Who are you and how have you managed to capture my heart so easily?"

"Like most people in Los Angeles, I came west to find fame and fortune. I won a beauty contest as Miss Memphis...that's in Tennessee."

"Yes, I know," he laughed.

"It earned me a screen test that went nowhere but it did help me meet some people. One of them was Dusty Kincaid...he makes western movies."

"Yes, I know who Dusty Kincaid is. He's definitely not your type. You seem more the urbane type, not the girl hanging on the arm of a hick with a piece of straw sticking out of his mouth."

"Well, Dusty is very nice. Apparently he plays tennis occasionally with Neil Pastore. That's how he was invited and you know the rest of the story. And you...what got you invited?"

"Neil and I are partners in an apparel company. He's the money and the mouth...I'm the suave creative one. It's a marriage made in hell."

"Then why did you do it?"

"I needed his money and credit line. It's a long story."

"I've got time," she said, having barely touched her drink.

"Are we going to your place or mine?" Charlie smiled.

"Neither tonight. You're taking me back to my car, kissing me chastely on the cheek, and asking me if I'm free next Saturday," she chuckled, beginning to stand.

"And why would I do that?"

"Because I intrigue you."

And she did! For the first time since Jessica left him and Pablo died that he had something besides Starlet in his life. Bunny noticed the change before anyone else.

"I've asked your opinion on the rayon group and all I get is 'you decide.' Is this the Charlie who won't even let someone else decide whether we need number two pencils? What gives, Mr. Barron? Have you stopped caring or did you finally decide others had valid opinions as well?"

"I trust you, Bunny," he said, his mind on his upcoming date with Ruby.

"You've met someone, haven't you?" she laughed. "You've actually met someone who's messing with your head."

"Fuck off," Charlie smiled. "Get the line ready. We need to get these samples out."

"Not until you tell me her name."

"Ruby...Ruby Taylor, now go to work."

"Knowing you, you probably got an erection just telling me her name," Bunny laughed, ducking as he threw a discarded doughnut at her.

"Damn her," he thought, readjusting his pants. She'd been right.

Charlie picked Ruby up at her apartment in Santa Monica, just off Montana. She invited him in for a drink. The apartment was small but tastefully decorated with inexpensive Andy Warhol prints on the walls and brightly colored pillows on the couch. Sinatra was singing discretely in the background.

"You have good taste," he said, walking around.

"On a budget," she replied, coming up next to him. Charlie could smell her perfume...subtle but definitely her.

"It's Givenchy, if you're wondering."

"He may have created it but you make it special."

They drove up the coast to Toscana, a small Italian restaurant in Zuma. Half the tables were empty.

"What made you decide on this place?" Ruby asked.

"I didn't want to overly impress you," Charlie smiled. "I just wanted somewhere quiet where we could get to know one another."

Ruby nodded and sipped a Chianti Charlie had ordered. Most of the restaurant's dim light came from empty wine bottles now holding lit candles. Oil paintings of Venice, Florence, and Capri adorned the walls and the owner, an old world host, wandered the tables, making sure the food was right and his customers were satisfied.

"How is Dusty these days?" Charlie asked.

"I broke up with him the day he returned from New Mexico. He wasn't happy."

"He's always got his horse to snuggle with. What made you end it so abruptly?"

Ruby didn't answer but her look said it all. She was as intrigued with him as he was with her.

They lingered over dinner and finished another carafe of wine. They held hands as they left, promising the owner, Signore Signorelli, that they would return.

Without a word, Charlie followed his date into her apartment, closed the door, and they kissed...a long lingering message. It spoke of deep feelings and a hope that this was serious. They undressed one another and moved under the covers, holding tight against the world.

Their hands moved slowly, like a blind person memorizing each curve and anxious to discover the person they were falling in love with. Ruby's nipples grew hard, and she could feel moisture between her legs as Charlie came erect and pressed against her. Their hands were everywhere, tender...caressing, and when he entered her, they were both ready, silently hoping this would never end.

They lay there together...spent, whispers of light drifting in from the other room, strains of another Sinatra ballad fading in and out. They made love a second and a third time before falling asleep, still clutching one another.

Charlie left for New York the following week. His days were filled with showing the line, schmoozing with friends and trying to make new contacts. He was in his element. This buyer got promoted to VP of Merchandising, this one moved to another chain for more money...another got fired for taking kickbacks.

Several New York manufacturers had started divisions with their version of a California look. One company Charlie took particular note of was called California Cooking run by Will Duval. It seems he had turned Ariana over to someone else so he could move to the West Coast...same partners, but a fresher look to the line. Will had clearly instructed his designer to think Starlet Fashions but make it better.

Word on Seventh Avenue was that the new company was being backed by one of the New York 'families' and it would be wise to check it out...very carefully. Charlie wandered around the 1411 building during Market Week.

He and Charlie made periodic eye contact but neither man made any attempt at conversation until Charlie's last day in New York.

Charlie had worked hard to open up a new account with a small chain of twelve stores in Oregon called Fred Meyer. They'd tested Starlet a year earlier and it had sold well. Charlie had explained that the Starlet team was the same group as before, just better capitalized. Their Buyer, Teddy Domici, had written him a sizeable order. Two days later Teddy called him.

"Charlie, Teddy Domici here."

"Hi Teddy, how's it hanging?" Charlie said cheerfully.

"I need you to cancel the order I gave you the other day."

"Cancel? The entire order? Why?" he said, shocked.

"Internal reasons. I'm sorry."

"Wait a minute, Teddy. There has to be more than 'internal reason.' What gives? Is there someone up the line I can talk to?"

"Drop it, Charlie. The order is cancelled. I'm sorry. I've got to run," Domici said, hanging up before Charlie could learn more details.

Within hours Charlie discovered what had happened. Will Duval had actually threatened the young Fred Meyer buyer if he didn't cancel Starlet's order and replace it with goods from California Cooking.

Charlie alternately turned pale and then red with anger. He stormed into the California Cooking showroom three floors below and interrupted Will showing the line.

"You son-of-a-bitch. You threaten a buyer…you actually threaten a buyer that if he doesn't cancel an order he's placed with me you'll harm him. You cocksucker."

Three women buyers looking at the line moved to the far corner of the showroom but they were too caught up in the drama to leave.

"You shouldn't storm in here, Charlie. I merely suggested that we had a better product at a lower price. The man agreed he had given you an order without properly evaluating his alternatives."

"Is that the way it's going to be, Will? You're going to 'suggest' your way into building a business. You can't compete honestly. You make shoddy goods and threats may help you get into a store but they won't keep you there."

"Charlie, I'll give you one threat. If you ever storm into my showroom again, it will be your last threat," Will said menacingly. "Now get the fuck out of here."

Time froze as both men stood, openly despising one another. Each of them barely containing their desire to lunge at the other until a woman in a corner of the showroom cleared her throat and the moment passed.

Each evening, despite the day's highs and lows,

Charlie would call Ruby, disregarding the cost of the long distance calls. For the first time, he had no desire to see other women. Meanwhile Ruby spent her days auditioning for any sort of role mentioned in Variety. She did an occasional commercial or walk-on and took acting classes. She had difficulty focusing, her mind drifting constantly to thoughts about this new man in her life.

Charlie and Ruby had morphed into becoming a couple and spent most nights at his apartment or hers. Their life was beginning to have a predictability that suited them both.

They married that September and drove to La Jolla for a quiet honeymoon.   Neither of them wanted a large wedding but a dozen friends including Bunny and Bruce Goslin were in attendance. They returned to Toscana for a celebratory dinner. That night Signore Signorelli closed his restaurant to other guests.

By December, Starlet Fashions was ready to close the year with a profit and both Neil and Charlie were pleased enough to give small bonuses to all the employees. More importantly, Ruby was pregnant. The year was going to end well.

seven

Fred & Tammy

Catherine Ann Barron came out howling...red as a beet and ready to take on the world. She had her mother's green eyes and fingers that never stopped moving. Within days she was smiling happily. Charlie breathed a sigh of relief, glad to bury the memories of his last pacing of a hospital floor.

Charlie had paid off most of the money he owed and felt confident enough for him and Ruby to buy a home in Encino, an upscale enclave in the emerging San Fernando Valley. It was south of the boulevard, the realtor had explained. She said that was important for property values but he never figured out why.

Ruby was thrilled. It had been an easy pregnancy and Charlie was loving and solicitous. Their daughter weighed just over six pounds and once she could suckle on her mother's breast she cooed contentedly. Her long curled fingers gripped her mother's hand and she showed the beginnings of light brown hair. The Barron's new home was beautiful, far grander than anything Ruby had seen growing up in Tennessee. Her mother, Myrna, came out on the train to help with the baby and, if her father could get vacation from his telephone company job, he'd visit as well.

I'm a father, Charlie thought, driving to work. Katie, his already nickname for his daughter, is beautiful. Fortunately, she has her mother's beauty. The thought of mother and daughter in matching Starlet outfits made him smile but took

his mind off his driving. The driver next to him blared his horn as Charlie drifted dangerously into the man's lane. He waved his hand in

apology. The other driver responded by extending his middle finger.

"Charlie, congratulations," Neil said, sitting in Charlie's chair when the new father arrived.

"Thanks...now get out of my chair."

"Of course," Neil said politely, "but we have to talk."

"What about?"

"There's money missing."

"What are you talking about? We made a profit. We should both be happy."

"It should have been a lot more. Did you sell off some of the garments without letting me know?"

"Are you kidding me?"

"That's not an answer."

"Look, I'm not unreasonable," Neil said, maintaining his calm. "I expect a little bit of cash to move around but this is too much. You're being a 'chozzer'...a pig about it."

"I sold off a few of last season's tops that were hanging...no big deal. I spent most of it on employee birthday cakes."

"Ten thousand dollars missing is more than a few hangers and birthday cakes. Listen, shmuck, you owe me five thousand dollars and an apology."

"You're crazy...how the hell did you come up with such a bullshit number?"

"Because I have accountants! Do you think I just sit on my ass? They ran your figures and then I made them run them again because I didn't think you were that kind of a partner. I know you gave up sniffing coke and you got married and had a daughter...all good stuff, but to cheat a partner is not good stuff. And to cheat me in particular is fucking suicide. You hear me?"

"Neil, what I'm telling you is, I maybe got an extra grand...nothing more...maybe a few hundred damages and samples I sold off in total. If more is missing, then we've got to look elsewhere."

"You telling me the truth?"

"On my daughter's life...I swear it. I may do some dumb things but I wouldn't rape this business...it's going too well."

"Then where is it?" Neil asked. "The damn garments didn't walk out on their own."

"I don't know but I'm sure as shit going to find out. If

messing with you is suicide, then messing with me is going to be worse."

Charlie attacked the problem systematically. He understood every part of his business. He had earned his graduate degree on the job and he was pissed. He would go through the paperwork in sequence. First fabric, then production and, finally, garments themselves. It took three weeks of working evenings to figure out what was going on...three weeks of checking cutting tickets...what went to the sewing contractors...how many garments were supposed to be produced and what was actually received.

On the surface it all seemed to check out. The fabric inventory checked out as well. How many yards were received, how many yards were required for each garment, how much fabric was still in inventory. The only thing left was finished garments ...what was being shipped and to whom.

Fred Solenger was the shipping manager. He'd been around the industry for decades and had come to Starlet for less money than he earned in any of his previous jobs. Charlie was never quite clear why or what happened at the company he'd worked at before. No one had bothered to check his references. Starlet needed a shipping manager and Solenger seemed to know his way around.

Then Charlie found it. It was in the UPS shipping records. There were hundreds of paper slips to go through but when he saw it, he knew. His shipping manager was sending one box every day to a fictitious company in

Lomita...a dozen or so garments every day, five days a week. It mounted up.

"It's Solenger, our shipping manager," Charlie said, this time sitting in Neil's office.

"Find a replacement. Don't say anything. Just make sure the new guy can start next Monday. I'll take care of our light-fingered friend."

Charlie didn't ask any of the details. He didn't want to know. His experience with Saul Rubenstein being killed had been a lifelong lesson. Sometimes the less you know, the better.

Fred Solenger left work as usual on a Friday afternoon, telling everyone he was going to go to Las Vegas for the weekend. He never returned to work but a few days later, a truck delivered several hundred garments back to Starlet.

"Mel," Charlie said to Mel Tibbets, his Production Manager. "I'd like you and Bunny to help me find a new Shipping Manager. Fred isn't working here anymore."

Charlie walked away quickly before he could be asked for more details.

Some woman, likely Solenger's girlfriend, called repeatedly over the subsequent weeks, looking for him, but Fred Solenger had vanished like a puff of smoke. Weeks later his car was found, a charred wreck, off a deep chasm in the Cajon Pass. There was no body.

"Have lunch with me," Neil said. "I'll meet you at Super Fish on San Pedro...one o'clock."

Charlie walked through the crowded restaurant, stopping to shake hands with friends or familiar faces. Super Fish was a popular haven in the industry.

"What's the occasion?" he asked, sitting down. Neil was already nursing a Perrier with a slice of lime in it.

"My way of apologizing for thinking you'd been a 'gonif.'" Neil loved to throw around Jewish expressions. Charlie thought the man pulled them from his ass. Pastore was one of the worst Jews he knew.

"Actually I was impressed your people could figure out money was missing, so it worked out well for us both," Charlie smiled.

They chatted casually about family and the industry.

"Hey," Neil said. "I need to find a new Los Angeles sales rep. If you know of any good ones, tell them to call me."

"What happened to Jay Stark? Isn't he your L.A. man?"

"Was! The IRS got him. Sentenced him to six months and a hefty fine. I doubt he'll come back to the business."

"Jesus! What for?"

"They figure he was stoned when he gathered his figures for the IRS audit and listed his drug supplier as a business expense...Eighty grand...the man snorted away nearly a third of his gross. Good thing you got clean ...could have been you."

Charlie's life was enjoying a plateau. He had a beautiful wife and the cutest daughter in the world. Starlet was doing well and his partner was leaving him alone. It couldn't last.

Fidelity was a struggle for many men. For Charlie it was an unnatural state...not only unnatural, but unnecessary.

Tammy King was hired to design a line for the Junior market. Bunny wasn't happy to give up part of her job but deep down she knew she couldn't do justice to the two very separate markets. The Junior market was trendy...hip, and sized for younger, slimmer women. Bunny's expertise was the moderately priced Missy market, where adapting expensive fashions was important and she knew that she did it as well as anyone.

Tammy was young and energetic. She could have modeled as a California surfer chic...a blonde Annette Funicello. She'd graduated with honors at the Fashion Institute, worked for two or three companies where she might have stayed until Charlie offered her considerably more money.

He also found it impossible to avoid her sexual energy. Tammy would come to work late, wearing leotards, perspiring from her workout at the gym and exuding endorphins in her wake. Bunny thought it was disgusting, but Charlie gushed at the vibes she sent his way.

The moment Tammy arrived at work each morning, she contrived to sit down in Charlie's office, her legs spread apart, drinking some sort of energized drink and chatting about the party she'd been to the night before, the movie premiere she was going to attend, and the latest trends in colors, styles, and sex. Charlie was smitten.

Starlet had moved to larger quarters and increased its staff. Cash...tax-free 'green,' flowed into Charlie's office from the sale of leftover fabric and garments that had been produced and not sold. He was careful, however, to divide the cash into equal parts for himself and Neil. Instinctively he knew what had happened to Fred Solenger and he had no intention of sharing the same fate.

Charlie suggested taking Tammy with him to visit The Limited, a hugely successful chain of boutiques located in Columbus, Ohio. Bunny took him aside and warned him...she knew the signs, but he just laughed.

"She's way too young for me," Charlie said, trying to sound mature. Bunny knew better.

"If she's been menstruating more than a year, you'll find a way to rationalize her age," Bunny said, smoking a cigarette, and walking away, shaking her head. Men...she thought. More often than not, they think with their peckers instead of their brains.

"Great line," the Limited's buyer gushed. "I think we can do good things with it. Can you promise me I won't see these styles at any of my competitors?"

"Definitely. As long as you can guarantee us enough of a quantity to dedicate a Cutting ticket, that style is yours," Charlie assured her.

Leslie Wexner sat in the corner watching his Buyer work. He had started the company with a $5,000 loan from his Aunt and built it into a national chain.

"Would you consider tossing in a $10,000.00 advertising offset if I double the order and agree to promote your label in our stores?" he asked.

Charlie had to restrain himself from getting on his knees and kissing Wexner's ring. It was an incredible offer.

"Absolutely! And congratulations on your success. I'm sure our companies will do good things together."

They walked out with the largest Purchase Order he'd gotten since he started the business. It was time to celebrate.

Charlie placed a call to the factory and spoke with Mel Tibbets, his Production Manager.

"Mel, get cranked up. We've got full cutting tickets and more on twelve different styles. I'll be back in a few days. Have someone call Neil and tell him."

"Grab your coat, Tammy, and I'll show you the limited sights of Columbus, Ohio...that's funny...limited sights...order from The Limited."

Tammy had been throwing herself at Charlie Barron since she'd taken the job. She even had a bet with three of her friends that she could make it happen before the 4th of July weekend. She'd won by two weeks. Charlie thinks he's seducing me, she thought. If he only knew. They had reserved separate rooms at the local Marriott but her room was never used.

She was young and nubile and for the first time ever Charlie felt overmatched. She was ready to try positions that required being an acrobat and Charlie worried about throwing out his back. By the time they were ready to fly home two days later, he thought he'd need a visit to the chiropractor to realign his joints and then sleep for a week. Tammy had brought a few joints with her and he was amazed how prepared she was.

A week later Charlie had developed an itch in his groin that wouldn't go away. He was afraid to get near Ruby and she was beginning to wonder why. He needed to get this checked out.

"You've got crabs, Charlie...good old fashioned crabs," the Doctor told him.

"Crabs? You have got to be kidding?" Charlie gagged, his eyes wide in wonder. "How the fuck would I get crabs?"

"Sexual intercourse is the most common cause but it can come from using a public lavatory, even from close but random contact. Any of these apply to you?"

"Not that I can think of," he lied. "What do I tell my wife?"

"I'll give you a prescription for some powder. It should clean things up in a few weeks but don't have sex with your wife until it's cured or you'll likely pass it on to her."

"Ruby, I'm embarrassed to tell you but I've got crabs and that's why I haven't come near you since I returned. The doctor has given me some powder. It will all be gone in a couple of weeks...pretty weird, right" he said, hoping she'd agree with him and not pursue the subject. He wasn't quite that lucky.

"Charlie...Charlie...who was it?" she asked, shaking her head as she sat, brushing her hair.

"No one, Ruby. I must have gotten it using a bathroom somewhere."

"Right! If that's the story you want to tell me, OK, but I want you to know the odds of it coming from a source other than screwing are pretty small. So, are you going to tell me? Who was she?"

"Ruby, I love you. I wouldn't cheat on you," he said, feigning every tone of innocence he could muster.

"Alright, Charlie. But one thing before I have to feed Katie, I don't know which is more disappointing...the fact that you had sex with another woman or the fact you've chosen to lie to me." He could see Ruby's shoulders droop as she left the room.

What an asshole, I am, he thought.

"Neil, it's time that I own 50% of the company," Charlie said, pacing his office, as Neil slid the cape from his shoulders and poured himself a drink from the half-filled carafe of 18-year old Glen Fiddich sitting in the corner.

"Certainly," Neil said, looking at Charlie's recent pictures of his toddler daughter. "Little Catherine looks like a very happy child, Charlie. Do you and Ruby plan to have others?"

"Let's keep the 'how's your family shtick' for another time, Neil. This needs to be resolved."

"OK. Let's resolve it. We shipped a little over Five million last year and netted nearly a half million. Ten percent of that is $50,000. Pay me $50,000.00 and I'll transfer ten percent ownership over to you."

Charlie gasped. "You Italian mother-fucker! You know that wasn't our deal. I've busted my ass to build this company while you sat back and took the cash envelopes without so much of a 'thank you' or a 'good job.' Now you want to renege on our Agreement. I'll see you in hell."

"Charlie, Charlie, calm down. Perhaps you need to read the Agreement more closely. It always said that you would need to buy equity at a fair market value. Didn't you read the Agreement...didn't your Attorney explain it?"

"Get out of my office...now, before I do something I'd prefer not to do."

"Suit yourself," Neil said, grabbing his cape, downing the last of his Scotch and exiting.

"Tom, I just had a meeting with Pastore," Charlie said to his lawyer, Tom Snyder, on the telephone. "He tells me our Agreement says I need to pay him to buy the 10% that would make us equal owners. Is that true?"

"It's true, Charlie," Tom replied. "I remember that section very well. I tried to discuss it with you two or three times but you didn't want to deal with any of it. You just wanted the Agreement signed."

"Fuck," Charlie said, pounding his fist on the desk. He really didn't care what the Agreement said at that time as long as he could get back in business.

"Is there any wiggle room?"

"Not much. It's a pretty simple formula."

"Well, as of now it will take $50,000.00 to make me an equal partner and I don't have that kind of extra dough sitting around. The other problem is that the more successful Starlet becomes, the more it will cost me to be an equal owner. In other words, the better I do, the more I'm fucked."

"Will the bank lend the money you need so you can buy in now? If they won't, you know there are those other options. I'm not recommending it but if you have to...you have to."

"The bank won't lend it and I'd get an ulcer if I needed to borrow from those sharks again," he said dejectedly. "Anyway, thanks Tom. I should have listened to you more carefully."

The knowledge that it would take $50,000.00 to equalize his ownership sat like a thorn in the paw of a wild animal. Charlie couldn't be at Starlet working without thinking about it. Even at home, he became more irritable. There had to be a way to find that money.

"Charlie, is everything alright?" Ruby asked. "Half the time you're at home, you aren't."

"I'm sorry, I really am. We need a vacation, that's what we need. Let's go skiing. I haven't been skiing in nearly two years. Maybe you can find someone to take care of Katie or we can take her with us."

"Can we ski another time? I'd really like to see my parents. My father still hasn't seen the baby."

"Skiing or Memphis, skiing or Memphis," he said, lifting his hands as in a balance scale. "Which would I rather do?"

Guilt won out! His affair with Tammy still cast a pall over their life.

"Why, Memphis, of course," he smiled. He was rewarded with a look of love that had been absent since he, Tammy, and his crabs returned together from Columbus.

Charlie and Ruby had been scheduled to take a connecting flight from Dallas to Memphis but their plane from Los Angeles arrived late...too late to make the plane. The Barron's had now been traveling nearly twelve hours and all three of them were cranky when the cab reached the Taylor home in a Memphis suburb.

"Hi, Myrna," Charlie said, kissing his mother-in-law on the cheek. "And you must be George. Mr. Taylor, nice to finally meet you." He looked at his in-laws and swore they must have been the models for Grant Wood's American Gothic poster...simple, plain folks sans pitchfork.

"So, this is my granddaughter. No offense, Charlie, but she does look like her mother."

"No offense taken, sir."

"Ruby, your brother, Henry, may drive over tomorrow from Knoxville," Myrna said without taking a breath. "He tried to open an office supply business last year but one of those big companies came into town and he couldn't compete. He and Millie are struggling, especially with two little ones. I'm not sure how they're going to survive."

Myrna had made a meatloaf and 'fixins' but the Barrons weren't hungry. They were eager to get to sleep. The time change had compounded their exhaustion.

Sunday morning, the Taylor family gathered for church. Henry's family had arrived late Saturday and the house was overcrowded, especially with a single bathroom. But there was no doubt that Catherine Ann Barron was the star of the show and was enjoying every minute of the extra attention.

Ruby had asked Charlie how he felt about their daughter being baptized and, once again, guilt triumphed over logic.

"Ruby, you know I'm Jewish. Maybe not a very religious one, but the idea of having my daughter baptized is tough for me."

"Charlie, I don't care either, but it will mean so much to my parents. Can we go through the motions and forget it when we get home...please?"

"You know I have no defense when you look at me like that but you're lucky we have no privacy in this house or you and I would begin work right now on getting Katie a brother."

"Charlie, I'd hate to think of it as work," she teased.

"Drudgery...absolute drudgery," he smiled. They both understood they had crossed the Rubicon...their marriage would be alright. She had forgiven him his transgression.

"...and in the name of the Father, the Son..." the Minister droned. Charlie couldn't bring himself to hold the baby over the Baptismal basin. Henry volunteered to do it while Charlie sat with the Congregation watching the proceeding.

Our young daughter is going to have heavenly protection from all sides, he thought.

"That was a nice thing you did, Charlie," George said that evening as he and Charlie sat alone in a living room where every upholstered piece of furniture had lace doilies protecting the arms. The room brought back memories of Charlie's impoverished childhood and of his mother, who had done the best she could with what she was given.

"Not a big deal," Charlie said, trying to minimize the event.

"Ruby tells me you aren't very religious. I've never really met a Jewish person. Oh, I've been introduced but I never had a chance to sit like this and I certainly didn't think we'd ever have one in the Taylor family. We've all been Baptists, going back as far as I know. Even had an uncle who was a Preacher...spell-binding man he was.

"Proves the world is changing, I guess. Next thing you know, the blacks will be demanding equality. Ever since that damn Parks woman decided she wouldn't give up her seat and move to the back on that Alabama bus a few years ago, there's been trouble. The blacks are organizing and the Klan is busy recruiting. There's sure to be blood spilled.

"Now I work with some colored folks and they're nice enough people but they're different and I don't mean just their skin color. I've even gone to their church and they've come to ours but that's about as far as I care to go, thank you," George said, as Charlie sat, startled by the rambling openness of his father-in-law.

"Is it very different in California, Charlie?"

"It is, George. We're more about getting ahead of the next guy and less about what he looks like or what color his skin is. We've got our racism and a number of neighborhoods that work hard to keep out Coloreds, Jews, Asians, Mexicans and anyone else that doesn't look like them or go to their church. But the Bible doesn't seem to control our everyday lives as much as it does with folks around here."

"Why can't people stay in their own neighborhoods?"

"If Ruby and I had stayed in our separate neighborhoods, you might have never had a granddaughter to Baptize today."

"Well, you're alright for a Jew-boy," George said, trying to make it sound light.

"And you aren't too bad for a crazy Southern Baptist," Charlie snapped back, tired of being patronized.

Charlie left the next day. Ruby and Katie would stay another week to visit but she understood that her husband couldn't get out of there fast enough.

"Thank you for letting me stay a little longer," she said. "Henry confided that neither my mother nor my father are healthy. He thinks my father might have prostate cancer. They're going to run tests and I need to be here to support them."

"Come home when you can. I'll miss you."

Charlie's fidelity didn't last any longer than Love Field in Dallas. He had gone to the American Airlines counter to upgrade his ticket for the leg to Los Angeles and met Ginnie...bright auburn hair, southern accent, and tits to die for.

She offered to upgrade him to the First Class cabin on the next morning's flight and he offered to reward her largesse with dinner. They both knew that the type of dessert they might enjoy would depend on the entrée.

They shared a slab of Southern bar-b-que'd ribs, licking one another's fingers, and laughing at the sauce covering both their mouths. They were on their third vodka when their hormones overwhelmed their appetite. Fortunately the restaurant and airport hotel were close to one another.

In the morning, Charlie strolled into the First Class cabin for his flight home.

eight

Mel Tibbets

"Andy...Charlie here...your old buddy. Meet me at Mike Lyman's and bring me some 'blow'...the good stuff. I've been celibate long enough. And, Andy...let's keep this just between us."

"Mel, I need to talk to you confidentially. Can we do that?" he asked, waving his Production Manager into his office and closing the door.

"Certainly, Charlie. What do you need?"

"A new costing arrangement. I'll make it worth your while. I want a dime added to the cost of every garment you have sewn. You arrange to have the Contractors pay that back to us under the table. Nobody's the wiser. I'll take eight cents...you take two. I think that's fair, don't you?"

"Sure, that's fair," Mel said, his mind wondering how it was fair at all but he'd be getting more cash under the table, tax-free, so who was he to complain.

Mel Tibbets was continuing to coordinate production and 'Papa' Edwards ran shipping. They were the team. They professed a loyalty to Charles Barron not unlike that of

Benedict Arnold cozying up to George Washington.

Charlie had figured out a way to amass the $50,000.00 he needed to pay Pastore the extra 10% he needed to become an equal partner in Starlet. It might take him a year or so but it would happen and the fucking wop wouldn't be able to lord it over him ever again.

There was something different about Charlie when he came to pick her and Katie up at the airport. He was energized, chatting and laughing. Maybe he's just glad to see us, Ruby thought, trying to convince herself of something she really didn't believe was the case.

"Everything OK, Charlie?" she asked as he drove the Buick north along Sepulveda Boulevard, Katie sleeping in her mother's lap.

"OK? Ruby, it's great. I got a call from the Vice President of Merchandising at Macy's. The bitch who has been keeping me out of their stores is gone and they want to talk about doing business. Starlet is going to break new sales records this year. So what do you think? Shall we go home and begin work on getting a brother for Katie?"

"If you're sure we're ready for another child. It's all so exciting...and I have missed you."

Ruby made small talk the rest of the way home. Her father's tests were negative but her mother had a spot on her lung. It was good to see them again but she no longer felt at home in Tennessee...and most important, she really hated it when she and Charlie were separated.

"I have a confession to make," she said nervously.   "I gave Henry $500.00 before I left.   He was sounding desperate. I hope that's OK."

"Sure...of course.   That's what families do.   They help one another," he said, glad her transgression was so minor.   He wondered if by some quirk of fate she and Katie had met Ginnie in the Dallas airport and compared notes. He shuddered at the thought.

Charlie worked hard at being faithful and domestic through the summer and fall.   Weekends he and Ruby would take Katie to the zoo or a museum. Business went on with the usual panics...fabric arrived full of damages, a chain in Detroit filed for bankruptcy, an employee was caught stealing, INS agents had gotten more active in raiding contractors and deporting illegals.   But Starlet escaped...unscathed.   Meanwhile, Neil and Charlie kept their distance from one another.

But across that part of the city that focused on garment manufacturing, rumors of sewing contractors and local manufacturers being threatened, spread.   These rumors couldn't be verified...until a shotgun blast killed one of the contractors.

La Femme was one of the city's larger sportswear manufacturers.   To improve their production they had decided to work only with large sewing contractors they could rely on.   It made sense until violence struck.   An unknown man walked into the factory of Armand Karokian, an Armenian entrepreneur, and, in front of men and women bent over 90 sewing machines, pulled out a shotgun and fired a double blast. Karokian died instantly, leaving behind a wife and three young children. His factory was closed. It never reopened.

In Long Beach, the financial manager of La Femme...the man who had thought up the idea of eliminating small contractors, barely escaped when a bomb planted under his car exploded. In fear of his life, he packed a small suitcase and disappeared. No one was ever caught.

Charlie thought of Will Duval and his friends. It seems his backers were doing more than just financing Will's garment company. They were no longer silent partners and the police were struggling to deal with it. Mickey Cohen and his associates had passed from the scene. With the help of Lana Turner's daughter, Mickey's bodyguard, Johnny Stompanato, had been killed as well. Even the Dragnas were gone from the scene, dying in 1956.

Someone else was running things now. Who, he didn't know, but Starlet would always be at risk from Duval. It was something he had never discussed with Neil Pastore.

As a new year lay ahead, Charlie's 'itch' returned. You can only carry this fidelity thing so far, he told himself, and Ruby's pregnancy had turned her attention elsewhere.

"Ruby, a few of the guys are going skiing in Aspen next week. I'd like to join them if you and Katie are OK without me."

"Absolutely...enjoy yourself. You've been working like crazy lately. It'll do you good to get away. Just promise you won't break a leg."

Charlie laughed and kissed her. That night he was especially attentive in making love and Ruby climaxed three times.

"My God...it felt like my pupils had left my eyes and floated into the top of my head. Whatever you did...write it down so you don't forget it.

"Ginnie...Charlie here. I'll meet you in Aspen late Thursday afternoon. You know where. Yeah...me, too. Ciao!"

"Here, you might want this before you go...last week's production," Mel said, handing Charlie an envelope. Nearly a thousand dollars of crisp one hundred dollar bills were inside. The two men smiled at one another.

He must take me for a simpleton, Tibbets thought. If he could up the labor costs a dime, why not fifteen cents. He was now taking home almost as much as Charlie, he laughed to himself.

"Andy...Mel here. Meet you around the corner at the taco truck in fifteen minutes."

Ginnie was waiting in the condo Charlie had rented. It was cozy inside, a small fireplace crackling comfortably. Outside the temperature was in the mid-20's and forecast to drop to the teens overnight, dropping another half foot of fresh snow. Charlie strutted in, masculine, horny, and filled with an energy enhanced by sniffing a few lines of blow at the airport.

Ginnie popped the cork from a bottle of champagne but he took only a single sip before taking her in his arms, lifting her up, and carrying her into the bedroom while she laughed at his outrageous behavior.

"Auburn really is your natural color. I would have bet money and a bottle of Clairol that it was something else but you have 'a snatch to match,'" he said crudely.

"This isn't the first time you've seen me naked," she said, nestling into the crook of his arm and throwing her leg over his naked torso."

"First time in the daylight. You are beautiful. Does American Airlines know what a treasure you are?"

"Not really...they keep me on the ground."

"My ex-wife was a stewardess. She loved it...got to travel all over."

"Why did you get divorced?

"We lost a child and I couldn't keep my pants zipped."

"I'm sorry about the first and I already knew about the second. It's why I'm not flying. I've got a Supervisor who says he's in a loveless marriage so we connect a couple of times a month. In exchange, though, I get lots of perks...time off, free flights...things like that. The arrangement got me here to Aspen."

"Well, I'll have to thank him. For the next few days though, he, my family, and my company are all off-limits. Come, blow me...it'll be a great way to begin the weekend."

"I feel wonderful this morning," Charlie said, pulling back the drapes to reveal a sun-filled sky against white snowy mountains. "I'm anxious to get some skiing in, how about you?"

"I'm a double black diamond kind of a girl. I doubt you'll be able to keep up with me...especially given your age," Ginnie laughed.

"I didn't hear you complaining about my age last night. If memory serves me right, you conked out long before I did."

"I was just being nice. I didn't want you to overexert yourself."

"Funny! OK, we'll compare notes at the end of the day. First one to the top of Walsh's Run buys drinks."

"Charlie...Charlie Barron, is that you?" a man shouted as he stood at the top of the cornice, catching his breath in the thin air and watching the chairlift arrive and drop its passengers.

Charlie and Ginnie had gotten separated and he turned to see who was shouting his name.

"Charlie...over here," a man waved his ski pole and snowplowed over. It was Alan Sentry, J.C. Penney's Los Angeles Merchandising Vice-President. Christ, thought Charlie, just what he needed. If anyone had a mouth that jabbered from the beach to Riverside, it was this guy.

"Hi Alan, surprised to see you here."

"I know. An old fart like me still churning the slopes. My wife and kids are around here somewhere. They insisted we vacation together as a family before my eldest daughter returns to college. Oh, here comes my wife. We got separated in the lift line. Brenda...over here," he waved, as a well-decked out middle-aged woman skied over. "You remember, Charlie Barron, don't you?"

"Hello Brenda," Charlie said amiably. "It's been a while."

"Charlie, good to see you," she said, not quite as amiably. Charlie's reputation for entertaining male executives was as legendary as his prowess with the women buyers and all the wives who had been around for more than a few seasons were leery.

He needed to get away before Ginnie arrived. She'd find him soon. They had agreed to meet at the top of the run.

"Charlie...wait for me," Ginnie shouted, rushing over, her chapped rosy cheeks lighting up her entire face.

Alan and his wife turned, watching the attractive young girl with the fashionable outfit ski towards them.

"Lost you somewhere around the mogul field," she laughed. "Oh, you've met some friends."

"Alan, Brenda, this is my friend, Ginnie. Ginnie...Alan and Brenda are from Los Angeles. They're up skiing with their daughter."

"How do you do?" Alan volunteered. "Do you live in Aspen?"

"I wish.   No, I live in Dallas.   I'm just up for the weekend." She could sense Charlie's discomfort...she was no fool. "I met Charlie at dinner last night and he said he'd show me some of the runs I wasn't familiar with."

Good girl, Charlie thought, breathing a little more easily. But one look at Brenda and he knew she wasn't buying it.

"Perhaps you'd both like to join us for dinner," Brenda smiled. She was clearly hopeful of learning more.

"Sorry, guys, but I'm already committed," Charlie said hurriedly, unsure of what Ginnie might say. "Besides, I'm getting cold standing around. I'm going to shove off. Nice seeing you all."

He pushed off, missing the trail completely and hitting a patch of ice. He lost his balance and fell as his friends watched. They skied over to him as a group.

"Are you alright?" Ginnie asked, trying not to appear overly concerned.

"Fine...stupid me," he said, standing and brushing off the snow. "I'm out of here."

The three of them waited, watching him get smaller in the distance and finally disappearing over a knoll.

"I'm through for the day," Ginnie said.   "Back to the lodge for me. Nice to have met you both."   She was gone before they could reply.

Alan and Brenda looked at one another with the knowing glance of a long married couple.

"You think?" she asked.

"Probably," he smiled. "Ah, to be young again."

"So you could cheat on your wife, you old bastard." She didn't wait for a reply, pushing off downhill.

Charlie decided not to risk meeting anyone else the next day. Instead, he and Ginnie drove to Snow Mass, a more remote ski area twenty miles away. The conditions were perfect…fresh powder, afternoon sun, and a warm thirty-two degree day with very little wind. By the time they returned to the Condo they had enjoyed a delightful day of skiing in perfect conditions.

Charlie decided he needed a nap before going out for the evening. Ginnie had something friskier in mind and as Charlie lay on the bed wearing only his briefs and a T-shirt, beginning to doze off, she returned with a can of Reddi-whip, smiling and giggling.

For the next half hour, every time his eyes began to close, he heard the burst of whipped cream and felt it on his chest, in his mouth, and on his testicles. Each dollop was followed by Ginnie's tongue licking it off. He couldn't control his arousal and he finally gave in, returning the whipped cream experience. He finally drifted off thinking…wow, that's better than coke.

Monday morning they parted at the Aspen airport, Charlie looking around nervously, anxious to avoid his Los Angeles friends. He didn't. They were sitting at the other side of the lounge area. Brenda nodded but made no effort to engage him in conversation. Ginnie had already said her good-byes.   She was leaving from a different gate, an hour later.

Four months later, Ruby miscarried.

"We'll have another," Charlie said solicitously.   If he believed in a higher being he might relate it to his ski trip with Ginnie. Fortunately for him, he wasn't. He took extra time from work and spent more time with his daughter, convinced an investment in family time would be good for them all.

"I'm telling you that son of a bitch is cheating me," Neil Pastore shouted into the telephone. "I don't know how I know it...I just know it. I have a sixth sense about such things. It's an itch that can't be scratched. I don't know what the fuck I want you to do...you figure it out. That's what I pay you for.

"And don't let on that I suspect anything," he added, slamming down the receiver.

"Neil, the whole place can hear you," Georgia said, coming in as Neil tried to calm himself down.

"I'm not good being cheated, Georgia...not good at all. I'll fry that cocksucker if I find out I'm right."

Starlet Fashions had grown. It had survived the high mortality of a start-up. Bunny Saxon had gotten married, divorced, and remarried when she discovered she was pregnant. The current husband was an alcoholic fabric salesman always trying to push whatever goods he was trying to sell to his wife.

Bunny resisted. She'd buy small amounts of his challis prints to keep peace at home but it did little good. Whatever she bought wasn't enough and if he'd been drinking, which was his usual condition, he'd cry, saying she didn't love him.

They were raising their one son, and she loved the little guy deeply but she felt as if she really had two children. Her mother took care of their son during the day and Bunny worked hard, smoked continuously, and chug-a-lugged one bottle of Coca Cola after another. Starlet was the only place she felt in control of her space.

Following the crab incident, Tammy King had agreed to leave and find employment elsewhere. It turned out she hadn't even celebrated her sixteenth birthday when she and Charlie connected in Columbus. It took some money to encourage her to leave without calling the police and Charlie smoothed things over by finding her a job at another company.

Tammy's replacement was a Hong Kong Chinese Girl, May Wong. She was petite and wore her hair in a chignon that made her look fragile, but this oriental lady was made of a will of iron. She came complete with interpreter, Lili Han, who was her assistant, her gopher, and her alter ego.

Everyone suspected that May...pronounced 'my' spoke perfect English but the subterfuge allowed her to completely ignore anything with which she disagreed. This was generally everything anyone suggested.

The Junior line had been rechristened 'Starstruck,' and was doing well. May Wong was a decent designer but becoming well-known was her only goal and by the third season the label and hang tags were changed to read 'Star Struck by May Wong.' Bunny was furious and deeply hurt.

Bunny saw her Chinese counterpart as lazy and conniving. She hated the bullshit and constant chatter she didn't understand. On more than one occasion she found Lili or May nosing through her office, stealing sample garments or print swatches or copies of Mademoiselle and Vogue.

"Get out of my office, you thieving bitches. You want ideas...get them on your own. You aren't going to steal what I create," Bunny screamed one day, putting a heavy padlock on the door to her office. She complained to Charlie but he chose to ignore her tantrum as a cat fight.

Bunny was reasonably certain that Charlie and Miss Chinese bitch were having an affair. After she complained to Charlie and got no satisfaction, May Wong would smile at her in a way Bunny could only describe to herself as being told to 'fuck off.'

Even Lili Han was in on it.

"Good morning, Missy Saxon," she'd say, giggling like an idiot. "Miss Wong will be in late this morning...she have business night." Then she'd giggle again.

"Charlie...I'm thinking of leaving," Bunny said, tired of having to ignore how hurt she felt. "You hire another designer without consulting me and then you let her name go on the label without considering I might like the same treatment."

"Bunny, it isn't the same," he protested.

"Of course not…you and I aren't sleeping together," she raged.

"Except that once," he said, trying to smile and calm her down. "Anyway, it's over. May has resigned. Norma Kamali made her an offer to start her own division and she accepted. She didn't even say goodbye…her stupid minion handed me a note. She even took the bulk of her office samples with her…samples Starlet had paid for."

"And you thought screwing her meant she liked you. You thought you were her hero? Jesus, men are stupid," Bunny said, dropping into a chair, laughing so hard tears began to form.

"OK, Miss smart-ass, what now? Do we continue Star Struck or drop it?"

"Why drop it? We'll find another designer and until we do, I can handle both lines but if you ever fucking do this to me again, I'll create a hang-tag with a picture of your balls on it."

"You can never leave," Charlie smiled.

"Charlie, I've gone over the figures for the last quarter and our Gross Profit is down," Audrey said. She was Charlie's bookkeeper although Neil had hired her, wanting his own eyes watching the books. Audrey Milton was short, near-sighted and lived with her widowed mother. Her job, and taking her mother to the movies once a week, was her life. She took a bus to work and saved her money for what she was sure would be a lonely old age.

Meanwhile, Audrey was thorough and accurate in her record-keeping. She tried hard to keep her questions and answers regarding the business non-confrontational. She understood the two owners didn't like one another but she liked her job and the only way to keep it was to avoid taking sides...just the facts, ma'am...all she'd do is present the facts.

"Returns...markdowns?" he asked. "I know we had to give some markdown money to Sear's on the tank tops that didn't fit."

"No, they're what we'd expect. I can't be sure but it seems like the labor costs have increased. I checked with Mel and he says when the contractors get busy they up their prices a little and manufacturers have to compete to get their goods done on schedule."

"So, does he say that's what happened?" Charlie asked, satisfied that his partner in crime had given a logical answer.

"Mel doesn't say yes...doesn't say no. All he says is 'possible,' 'maybe,' 'could be.' He should have been a politician."

"Well, we're still profitable, right?"

"Sure, sales are good and operating costs are in line, so we're OK."

"Then let's move on and see how it looks next quarter," he said, easily, hoping his carefree response would satisfy Audrey and his partner. He now had nearly fifteen grand in green stashed in a safety deposit box.

"You showed these figures to Charlie?" Neil asked. He had closed Audrey's door and they kept their voices down. Charlie was at the Mart. Neil had no desire to arrive unannounced and anger his partner but he did want to see if anything amiss was going on.

"Of course! And, I told him what Mel Tibbets said. In the end Mr. Barron was pleased that sales were good and profits were up…"

"But not what you thought they should be," Neil interrupted.

"Not what you think they should be…don't put words in my mouth," the short bookkeeper said defensively. "I don't know if labor prices are up and if they are up, why. Why don't you ask them both?"

"Because I'm not ready to," he said, throwing the figures on the desk, grabbing his cape, and walking out.

It was the '70's before Ruby and Charlie had another child…a boy, Roger, entering the world at a little over seven pounds and twenty-two inches long. He was going to be tall. Ruby's parents were invited out for the bris and agreed to come after she sent them two prepaid airplane tickets. Charlie objected adamantly to having them stay in the house and Ruby reluctantly agreed that they would have to stay at a nearby hotel. He couldn't handle his bigoted father-in-law being underfoot twenty-four hours a day.

The Barrons had moved to a larger home further up the hill and higher on the social scale. They had also joined the Lakeview Country Club where they would host a dinner after the small family event.

"I wish my parents had lived to see this," Charlie said, as they were getting dressed. It was a rare moment of introspection.

"They would be very proud of you," Ruby said, coming over and planting a kiss on her husband's cheek. "Shlomo Baronski! Wow, that's a mouthful you never mentioned before I agreed to marry you. Mrs. Shlomo Baronski...wouldn't that have set my father back another century."

"Shlomo Baronski is long gone," he said, tying his tie.

"Well, the Rabbi says that tonight...and just tonight, that man is going to be resurrected when his new young son is given his Jewish name."

"And, tomorrow, with luck, he will go back in the suitcase of memories just as soon forgotten."

"Neil...Charlie! Listen," he said cheerfully on the telephone. It had a long, thirty foot cord and Charlie loved to walk around the office, pacing, while he chatted. "Satin...I need satin...heavy stuff...we're going to make satin jeans, lots of colors. No, I'm not crazy...just fucking brilliant," he laughed.

Disco was coming and people from teens to seniors were going to be dancing to light balls that reflected around the room and they would be dressing up for it. Crazes came and went but sometimes they lasted for more than one season. Saul Rubenstein thought he'd had a big one with the polyvinyl dresses but that had turned out to be a spike that vanished almost as soon as it came. This was different. This was John Travolta, Donna Duval, and the Bee Gees. This was date night and dancing and dressing up. This was going to be hot...Charlie was sure.

Charlie was eating lunch at Dale's in the Mart enjoying their famous Cobb Salad and chatting amiably with a few friends when Alan Sentry entered and Charlie's antennae vibrated. Alan never showed up without an appointment and usually demanded the same treatment accorded royalty. J.C. Penney gave their California buyers and merchandise executives a great deal of latitude in buying women's apparel and they demanded near-reverence in exchange.

"Hi Alan," Charlie said, wiping his mouth and putting down his fork. "Let me introduce you..."

"Charlie, I'm not happy," he interrupted, ignoring the others at the table.

"What did we do wrong or what should we have done that we didn't?" he said, trying unsuccessfully to lighten the situation, and sharing the embarrassment of his friends who couldn't figure out how to extricate themselves.

"Satin...fucking satin and disco. I missed it...Dallas missed it and the Corporate Merchandising Vice-President is really pissed at me."

"It came out of nowhere. I saw it at a couple of New York nightspots and I guessed it would spread. Who knew how right I'd be? Donna Summer...John Travolta... a whole new craze."

"Who indeed? I need to place an order...a good-sized order and I need delivery yesterday. Get an order pad," he ordered.

"That's our cue to leave," Charlie's friends said, dropping some money on the table and dashing away.

"Alan, I'm happy to take an order but we're out of fabric...everything we've got is already being cut against orders. We're probably talking ten weeks before I can get you goods, even if I bring all the fabric in by air. Let's go up to the showroom and continue this discussion up there."

"No way ten weeks. This thing could run its course by then. Latest I need is end of the month...that gives you four weeks at the outside," Alan said, showing no interest in going anywhere.

"Can't do. Alan, you know I'd never say no to you if there was any other way but I can't shit the fabric."

"Listen, you prick, my job is probably on the line. You will get me goods," Alan whispered. His face was getting red and his hands were beginning to shake.

Charlie had dealt with angry buyers before but the people from Penney's were usually reasonable.

"Let me try, Alan...let me try. That's all I can do."

"Sure, Charlie...you try, you try hard because if you don't get me goods I'd have to let your wife know about your friend, Ginnie, and I'd hate to do that, I really would."

Charlie was stunned. Fucking blackmail when he and Alan both knew that they'd each strayed on multiple occasions.

"Are you kidding me? You'd fuck up my marriage because your company didn't pick up on a trend? Have you guys sunk so low?"

"Not them, Charlie...me. I'm getting older and I have no desire to be on the street again looking for a job. You do this for me." He turned and walked out, knocking over a full tray of dirty dishes being carried by the busboy.

Near panic took over Starlet. Neil was brought in to scrounge for more fabric and existing orders were re-allocated to deliver short where they could, cancel specialty store orders and pay a premium for fabric and labor. They shipped on time against the JC Penney order, balancing anger from other stores against a revengeful Alan Sentry.

A few weeks later a contrite Alan Sentry stopped by the Starlet showroom. Charlie saw him out of the corner of his eye. He was showing a new line of dresses they were experimenting with to the Nordstrom's buyer. The woman, Lynn Moffett, a little older, had always shunned Starlet as being a little too main stream for them.

"Now these have the feeling I'm looking for, Charlie. How about a test order? If they check, we can try more stores."

"That works for me, Lynn," he said, smiling, but confused. He knew Alan was waiting to see him with a look of patience he'd never seen before. The memory of Alan's outburst at Dale's was too recent.

"Let's do dinner next time you're in Los Angeles."

"Thank you, Charlie. That would be nice," she said without nuance...without inflection. He understood that, to her, it was just a dinner invitation.

"Alan, nice to see you. I'm sorry to keep you waiting." He struggled to keep his voice and emotions even. He would never forget this man's threat. Men didn't do that shit to other men.

"Hi, Charlie. Don't worry about it. I have a problem and I need your help."

"Certainly!"

"J.C. Penney...my company...the place where I've spent the last fifteen years, is closing its Los Angeles office and centralizing all the buying for the entire company in Dallas.

They've told me I can either move to fucking Texas at a lower salary or take early retirement. I want to see what other options I have that will allow me to remain in Los Angeles.

"You know a lot of people and I was hoping you'd see if any of them were interested in an experienced buyer. Brenda has made it clear. If I move to Texas, she's going to stay here and get a divorce."

Charlie stared at the man. The absolute fucking nerve this guy had to ask his help. This over-the-hill son of a bitch was getting the karma he deserved.

"Absolutely, Alan. I'm glad to help. I'll put out some feelers and let you know. You're a staple here in the city and I'm sure you won't have any trouble finding a home. Now don't you and Brenda worry."

Alan managed a thin smile, shook his hand and thanked him.

Charlie watched him leave, took the resume Alan had left with him and tore it into small pieces.

Neil Pastore marched into Starlet with the confidence of General Patton storming Sicily.

"Good morning, Mr. Pastore," the receptionist smiled. "Can I help you?"

"No, I need to see Charlie."

"He's having a staff meeting and asked not to be disturbed."

"He'll be happy to be disturbed for me," he said, walking by and opening the door to Charlie's office."

"Neil, can't this wait?   We're having a production meeting."

"Sorry, folks. Have your meeting later. Charlie, this is important."

Charlie just stared at Bunny, Papa and the rest as they walked out. Neil closed the door behind him.

"I just got off the phone with some friends from the Italian-American Club I belong to. It seems someone figured out that the popularity of the Godfather movie means merchandising opportunities and I've arranged for Starlet to buy a license for Godfather women's sportswear. Fantastic, right?"

"Are you out of your fucking mind? That's a movie where the people look dowdy and go around killing one another. There isn't any fashion statement...any style."

"But it has great name recognition."

"So what. Why not buy a license for MASH? Then we could design a line of Army fatigues. Why didn't you ask me?"

"Because I own 60%, remember? That means I don't need to ask. Have Bunny figure out something? Target stores is coming into town next week to see what we've got.   They want to plan a big Godfather roll out...boy's, men's and even some kitchen items."

"Probably knives for removing a horse's head. Can we at least show Target the rest of our line? That would, at least, give this debacle some upside."

"Fuck you, Charlie. I come in here with a great idea to build our company and you shit all over it. Do whatever you want. You know, you're a real prick!" he said, pulling open the door and storming out.

Charlie sat there for a minute, just staring at his partner's exit and then he began to laugh, tears running down his cheek.   Godfather sportswear...talk about someone   not   understanding   the   women's   apparel business.

Three people showed up from Target stores the following week. They were all pleasant, soft-spoken merchandising executives. They'd flown in from Minneapolis and were staying at the Hilton.

"Welcome to Starlet," Charlie said, smiling his best and cheeriest look. "I'm hoping we have things to interest you."

Paul Devine was one of their Vice-Presidents.   Sarah 'something' and Barbara 'something else' were buyers. They were all dressed in conservative mid-west suits, ready for a blizzard that might strike at any time.

Charlie tried small talk for a while as coffee and soft drinks were offered. Bunny, meanwhile had move a rack of clothing in that had hurriedly been modified with a Godfather hang tag and label.

"Charlie, let me stop you," Paul Devine spoke up. "We haven't figured out whether we can make this Godfather name apply to a woman's line. Works fine for men's T-shirts so unless you've figured out a new angle, we can keep this meeting short."

Charlie smiled. "Thank goodness. We thought it might just be us. When my partner brought it to me I thought it was one of the dumbest ideas I'd ever heard. This is our designer, Bunny Saxon. She came up with a slant you might like."

"Instead of the violence and testosterone that was in the movie, we opted to play up the sexiness of Italian women. You know, Sophia Loren, Gina Lollabrigida...tight-fitting bodices, shorter skirts but nothing too over the top. We used warm colors spread across new print styles."

Her pitch flowed easily from one group to another. Charlie watched as their expressions moved from wary to accepting. They asked a few questions...sizes, SKU's, prices but nothing about the styles themselves. Sarah was hesitant to offer her opinion, deferring to the others.

Barbara blurted out first.   "Wonderful.   Isn't it wonderful, Paul? They've taken a dog of an idea and actually made it workable. With one or two exceptions I think we can blow these right out of the store."

"I agree.   Why don't you girls put an opening order together? I want to see some of L.A. This is my first time here," Paul Devine said, standing. He wasn't tall and he wasn't handsome but he was a presence.   He could definitely command a room when he wanted to.

"How about I play tour guide?" Charlie offered. "We can meet the ladies for drinks at your hotel later."

"Works for me."

The two men climbed into Charlie's Porsche and headed west.

"I like your car," Paul said. "I'd be afraid to be seen in something like this in Minnesota."

"There are still enough stretches in Southern California to open it up but they're getting crowded pretty quickly. How long have you been with Target?"

"Nearly fifteen years. They're good people and living in the Midwest has its advantages. Originally I came from the Bronx."

"No kidding. I was from the eastside."

"Yeah, my family were 'polacks'...strictly old country.

"We were somewhere in Eastern Europe."

"So Barron wasn't your family name?"

"Shortened it a long time ago."

They stopped for a drink and lunch at the Beverly Wilshire comfortable knowing they were both two guys who grew well beyond their origins. Their conversation stopped suddenly and Paul gaped as he noticed Jack Nicholson walking across the lobby. Charlie just smiled.

They looped around Santa Monica and returned along Sunset watching the handsome people shopping along the strip. By the time they returned to the Hilton the two men were fast friends.

"Thanks, Charlie. We've got nothing like this in Minnesota but if you come back I'll try my best to reciprocate."

"Paul, it was my pleasure. And, I'll take you up on that offer."

A few days later Charlie and Neil passed one another at the Mart. Neil gave a 'thumbs-up.' Charlie just smiled and stuck up his middle finger.

nine

Will

"Charlie, there's a woman out here to see you," Sandy said, speaking into the intercom Starlet had recently installed.

"Who is she?"

"She said to tell you it was Jessica."

Sandy heard Charlie's chair turn over and his door fling open.

"Jessica," he said, his mouth agape. "Oh, my God. Sandy, hold all my calls...cancel anything I've got the rest of the day."

Jessica smiled, a far different smile than Charlie remembered, and a million miles from the TWA stewardess he'd fucked in the airplane's tiny lavatory a lifetime ago.

"How are you? Can I get you something?"

"No, Charlie, I'm fine," she said, sitting down and gathering the blue print sari she was wearing around her.

"You look wonderful. My God, how many years has it been?"

"Close to ten, I think...maybe more. Time has a different

meaning to me now."

"Where have you been living?

"On an ashram in Topanga Canyon. You wouldn't like it. It's very communal, people come and go, and everyone shares. It's serene...very peaceful. I heard you remarried and have a daughter."

"And a son...yes, two children. And you, did you remarry?"

"Not in the Western sense...we are all married to one another."

"Sounds cozy," he smiled, hoping to rekindle the warmth they had shared.

"Not like that, Charlie. It's different."

"Well, I'm glad you're happy, Jess. You deserve it. Things might have been very different if our baby had lived."

"Yes, I've thought about that many times. It broke my heart. But then I thought it might be Krishna's plan for me."

"It's wonderful seeing you. You just disappeared. We had no closure, you and I...we left so many things unsaid. Now out of the blue, you're here and I'm thrilled. But you must have a reason. Why now? It's been so long."

"I need your help. You once said you would always care for me and I hope you still have those feelings. I want to travel to India, to make a pilgrimage, to bathe my soul in the Mother Ganges. It costs a great deal of money I don't have. I haven't needed money since we parted, but now I do."

"Have you asked your parents?"

"No, I have finally accepted that they are not nice people…they are filled with avarice; their souls are rotting."

"You've got that right," he smiled, remembering his bastard father-in-law and his vacuous wife. "How much are we talking about?"

"Three thousand dollars. I know it is a great deal of money and…."

"Of course. I owe you that…and more. Can you give me a day or two to put it together?"

"Thank you, Charlie. You are a good man," she said, standing to go.

"Where are you going? Don't leave! You've just gotten here and there is so much I want to know.   Can I take you to lunch? Maybe you could come to dinner…meet my wife and see the children," he rushed his words.

"No, but that's very sweet."

"Well, how can I get you the money?"

"The ashram will send someone to pick it up. Don't worry, it's entirely safe. And thank you, Charlie. Namaste!"

"Where the fuck is Mel? He's been gone the entire week and production is messed up.   Papa," he said to the shipping manager, "Any idea where he's run off to?"

The tall man, black as the ace of spades, and as smart as anyone who had grown up in the ghettos and survived the neighborhood gangs, knew to keep things to himself...it promoted longevity in life.

Abel Edwards was one of five children of a single mother. None of his siblings had the same father, just a mother with a perpetual optimism that some man would stay around long enough to help raise her brood. Abel tried, enough to earn him the nickname 'Papa' for his efforts to raise his younger brothers and a sister.

"No idea! I wish I could help, Charlie, I sorely do, but we need to find him and get those garments in here before their cancellation dates. We're already late on some key styles."

"Neil says you need to hire a new Production Manager...and quick," Audrey said, not caring that she was interrupting.

"Neil says? What the fuck does he know that I don't and why didn't he call me?"

"Ask him yourself. All he told me to tell you was that Mel Tibbets is history."

"Neil," Charlie shouted angrily into the phone. "Mel Tibbets? What's going on? A Porsche Targa? In his garage? Shit!"

Charlie understood immediately what had happened. Neil had confirmed his suspicions that money was being siphoned from the business.

"Sure, come over," Charlie said, exhausted and suddenly, very afraid.

It seemed like only minutes before Charlie heard his partner arrive at Starlet and storm into his office.

"The fucker was getting kickbacks from the contractors," Neil ranted.

"How did you find out?"

"Your friend, Andy, can have a big mouth when someone threatens to break his arm. It seems he's terrified of pain. I had a friend convince him to tell me who his clients were around here. I wasn't surprised he named you. I knew you've been back on that shit for a while now.

"I was surprised about Mel. When I checked further I found out he was placing a lot of bets on the horses and had this expensive car hidden in his garage, a car that my young daughter is really going to enjoy driving."

"Where is Mel now? I want to beat the shit out of him."

"No need. Someone has graciously taken care of that for us. Would you like to know the details?" Neil asked, a look of pure evil pleasure on his face.

Charlie remained silent. What more did Neil know, or suspect? He shook his head...better not to know.

"I warned you to stay away from that shit but it's your money so I can't stop you. You want it to fry your brain...that's your business, and your bimbo...what's her name? Ginnie? You keep thinking I'm a dumb WOP ...when will you learn? I could have been your friend if you'd let me but you've got this destructive side to you that will eventually crash our company. What a shame!" He walked out shaking his head.

Charlie got up and closed the door, his hands were shaking. He laid down two lines of coke, stared at it, and pushed the $500 worth of powder onto the floor. He laid his head on his desk and cried.

"Mr. Barron, are you alright in there?" Alice called on the intercom. "Mr. Barron, Bunny wants to come in?"

"Charlie, it's Bunny...can I come in? Charlie...please answer."

"Leave me alone...I'm fine. I just need some time alone."

It was nearly seven before Charlie stood and poured himself a drink. His hands were shaking as he tried to focus on the simple task of pouring scotch from a carafe into a glass. Everyone would be gone and be sitting down to dinner or stuck on a freeway somewhere.

He opened the door to the quiet and took a deep breath before returning to his desk and sitting down. He had barely escaped this time. What had Mel told them...had he implicated me? Charlie wondered. Did Neil know it had all been my idea and, if so, why wasn't I harmed?

"Charlie! Can I help?" Bunny said, softly, peering into his office. "I couldn't leave without knowing you were OK."

"I'm fine, Bunny. Thanks, but you shouldn't have stayed so late."

"I'm your friend...that's what friends do. Want to talk about it?"

"I don't think so...another time, maybe."

Andy was gone as well as Mel Tibbets. Rumor had it that Andy had scurried off to Colorado Springs after being threatened. He started driving a cab after he got clean of his own habit, thanks to a sister who took him in. There were no rumors regarding Mel.

"Charlie, we have a small problem," Papa said, catching the owner wandering through the hanging goods in the warehouse to see what he needed to close out.

"Why not?" he answered sarcastically.

"We've been asked to change to another company for our trash pickup."

"So? You tell them 'yes'...you tell them 'no.' I don't care."

"It's triple the price."

"Then tell them 'no.' "

"Ain't so easy. Dragna's people used to own this particular trash outfit. Same type of muscle they used twenty years ago and these guys aren't easy people to say no to."

"Hold 'em off...let me talk to Neil. Maybe he's got an idea."

"Neil, we can handle tripling the cost of our trash pickup but it puts these crooks in our backyard."

"It's going on all over town. Most companies are afraid to go to the police...some of the cops are probably taking kickbacks as well. I remember when the mob tried to unionize the sewing contractors but they didn't have a lot of luck. Most of the cutters and sewers are illegal aliens and these people are more afraid of Immigration than the mob guys. Trash is the mobs new tactic. Give it to them and let's hope they leave us alone for a while."

Since Mel's disappearance, Charlie waited, nervously, for any indication from Neil that he knew his partner was in on the kickback scheme. There was none but it was hard to not wonder. Meanwhile, with Mel out of the loop, Charlie's cash infusion had dried up. He'd have to play it straight for a while.

The new Production Manager Charlie hired, Sam Martinez, had come to Los Angeles from New York. Doctors had told him it would be better for his youngest son's asthma. He'd only been in California a short while and he was still learning which sewing contractors to work with. It would be months, maybe never, before Charlie would even consider broaching a kickback scheme with a man with whom he had no history.

Martinez's family was originally from Puerto Rico. He had a sharp, biting, wit and a perpetual smile that made some people nervous. Papa didn't trust him, and Bunny thought the guy was a complete ass.

Sam was convinced he could get the best prices in the city for labor. He'd bring doughnuts to the contractor's workers, chat with them in Spanish, ask about their families, explain how to get fake Green cards and identification, but he'd left his previous job under a cloud and no one knew what it was.

Sam would come into work Mondays, after spending time with his wife, Petra, and his two sons, flashing a wad of bills. His sons nine and twelve were in the El Monte Boy Scouts and Sam was an Assistant Scout Master. Everyone's interest was piqued. Where was all this money coming from? And then one of the young workers in the warehouse revealed Sam's secret...cock-fighting.

Sam Martinez trained cocks to fight and, in the back alleys of El Monte and Rosemead, crowds would come to bet on which bird could kill the other. More often than not, Sam's won and he pocketed a great deal more cash from the betting than he earned managing production for Starlet.

"At least he isn't a pervert," Charlie told Papa, when he learned what was going on.

"God bless to that," the huge warehouse manager laughed.

Will Duval sat quietly nursing a Perrier in the bar of the swank Beverly Wilshire Hotel. He was nervous...his palms were damp and he wiped them on a napkin.

"Will?" the heavy-set be-speckled man asked, as he approached. He was well dressed and exuded a soft pleasantness.

Duval was startled. He had been so deep into his own thoughts he hadn't seen the man enter the bar.

"Don't get up," the man said in a fatherly tone. "Let's move to a booth. More privacy! Thanks for meeting me. I got in from Vegas a little late last night...sorry to keep you waiting.

"I'm one of Mr. Sam Giancana's friends. Mr. Giancana died a few years ago but his organization continues to function and there is a business proposition I'd like to discuss."

"Not a problem," Will said, working hard to regain his composure.

"You run California Cooking, I understand. Nice goods. I have two daughters and they tell me it's 'cool stuff.' I guess that means it's good."

Will just smiled, not sure where this was all going.

"Let me clear the air. We've bought out your New York partners. Now we are all in business together."

Will stared as he tried to make sense of what he'd just been told.

"Can you tell me why?" he finally asked.

"Certainly. Our organization owns casinos in Las Vegas, although our primary businesses have always been in Chicago. From time to time we're going to want to move some money. We'll be moving it through California Cooking. You needn't be involved. We'll have our own financial guy at your place taking care of it. You have a problem with any of this?"

"No," Will stuttered. "I don't think so."

"Good. My friends said you were easy to do business with. And, if you need any help growing our business...let me know. My finance guy will be at your place next week. He'll know how to contact us. And if you want to come to Vegas, let him know and we'll see that you're comp'd. Think of it as a fringe benefit to our relationship. Nice to meet you...got to run. There's a lovely young lady waiting for me upstairs."

Will swallowed the remainder of his Perrier and motioned to the bartender.

"A Jack Daniels...make it a double!"

An hour later Will Duval was still sitting there. The mob in New York had always left him alone and he made sure he always had a stuffed envelope for them. They seemed satisfied, never complained, and if he'd taken a little more than they'd agreed to, they didn't seem to care.

These past few years he'd been three thousand miles west, far away from his partners, and able to run his own show. With that type of independence he was free to play any type of game he chose. It had been a most profitable interlude. Fortunately, until these past two seasons, the company had grown and he'd been able to keep their take at the same level, so life went on.

But now...double daggers...an in-house snitch to watch him and a business that's flat. He wasn't going to be able to avoid the first but he sure as shit needed to fix the second.

Pépe Castellano was strong and wiry for his size but that doesn't mean much when you stretch to five feet. Pépe had been a jockey at Aqua Caliente, a flea bitten track in Tijuana, Mexico, just south of San Diego. Three years ago he'd gotten a fake Green card and wrangled rides at Santa Anita. Most of his mounts were fillies, too young or too old to be serious contenders. They were included in the race to fill out the field.

Santa Anita was still far better than Aqua Caliente until he agreed to ride a nag in the Santa Anita Handicap. Pépe had been careless and let himself get sandwiched between two horses on the far turn coming into the straightaway. His left leg twisted...badly. The doctors fixed it so he could walk but it would always be with a limp and he'd never ride again.

That really didn't matter anyway. The racing board and the Jockey's Association had already decided to ban him from riding for betting on the outcome of the races he was riding in. Now, a year later, he was into the bookies for five large and they were getting impatient.

"Are you Castellano?" Will asked as he pulled his car to a stop at Olympic and Indiana Streets in East Los Angeles.

"Yeh!"

"Get in! Thanks for meeting me."

"I don't think I was given much of a choice."

Will looked at the smaller man sitting next to him but decided not to respond.

"Your friends thought you could help me. If you can, we can make your problem go away."

"Who do I have to kill?"

"Nothing quite so drastic. I'm hungry. Any good place for tacos around here?"

"Depends how strong your stomach is. Hang a right at the next block. Tito's...on the left."

They ordered and sat, staring uncomfortably at one another.

"You have a sister, Luisa..."

"She's my half-sister...different father."

"Whatever. She's the Production Pattern Maker at a company called Starlet Fashions.

"If you say so," Castellano said in a surly, get on with a 'how I'm going to get fucked' tone.

Again Will kept his calm.

"I want to know what new styles Starlet is going to produce...fabric, colors and prices...I definitely need to know their sell prices. Luisa brings me a pattern of the garment and all the information. Easy!"

"You want me to pimp garments for you? You've got to be kidding. I know horses. I don't know shit about women's blouses."

"Listen, asshole," Duval said, wiping salsa off his hands and finally confronting the ex-jockey. If you knew horses we wouldn't be sitting here. You're a loser and now your ass is mine. You do this and your debt goes away...you don't and you go away. Entiende?"

"I don't know if she'll help me. We aren't that close," he said in a sullen, contrite tone.

"Make it happen. We'll pay her...$100 for each style. No one needs to know."

When Will returned to his office there was a man waiting. He was sitting, nestling an old style leather briefcase. He was wearing a tired suit and wire-rimmed glasses. Will guessed him to be well past fifty but adding another decade wouldn't have surprised him.

"You are?" Will asked.

"Fred...Fred Stanton, but everyone calls me Uncle Fred. I think Mr. Giancana's associate might have mentioned that I'd be here for a while."

"You know anything about the garment industry, Freddie, like factoring, and that shit?"

"Mr. Duval, we're going to be together in a most intimate way and I find your tone terribly unfriendly. I suggest you reconsider your attitude or I will make your life hell. Now, where is my office?"

"My father is dying," Ruby said to Charlie that evening. "I've been on the phone much of the day with my brother. My mother is in no condition to have a rational conversation. I plan to take the kids out of school and fly out on Thursday. Will you come with me?"

"I can't, Ruby. It's impossible for me to leave right now. I fly to New York next Wednesday and the line isn't together. I wouldn't be very good just sitting around with your family but I know you should go. You can leave the children if you want. I'll get them to school."

"No, that's too complicated. I'll take them with me."

The chief buyer for Fashion Conspiracy, a chain of 150 boutiques spread out in malls around the country and headquartered in San Diego, was Sharon Morsey, whose reputation included devouring showroom sales reps for lunch. She was rarely satisfied and she had her own convictions on what her customers would buy...this color is wrong...that fit is terrible...these buttons are too small. Charlie's sales people couldn't deal with her. She was a bulldozer. It was a challenge Charlie couldn't resist.

"Hi Sharon, I'm Charlie Barron, I own Starlet Fashions. Thanks for coming in to look at our line."

"You're welcome, Mr. Barron. I can give you twenty minutes, and then I have an appointment on the Third floor."

"I'm afraid that won't be enough, Miss Morsey. Let's reschedule for another time," he said, knowing full well this time tactic was something buyers sometimes liked to do to take control of the give and take of showing a line.

She stared at him. This man won't intimidate. Their optic exchange hung in the air while Starlet's other sales people fidgeted. Sharon Morsey broke first.

"I'll reschedule my other appointment; show me what you've got."

Charlie nodded to Liz, his top showroom girl, who began to set out each group.

"No one else is showing muted colors, this season," Sharon Morsey noted, tossing aside an entire group of print blouses. Liz blanched and stared at Charlie, not knowing what to do next.

"Have you checked Neiman's and Sak's...the Designer departments? You're the boss, but I'd rethink your conviction," Charlie said, calmly.

She paused...saying nothing and staring at Charlie.

"You need to order these Korean silk tops," he added. "Their price will blow you away and we're the only company showing this fabric. We have an exclusive on it."

"What colors does it come in?"

"Give us at least a gross and you can have any color your heart desires…and you can mix it in different styles."

TEN

ʃharon

Sharon Morsey smiled as she finished writing up her order, including a large number of styles with muted colors. More than two hours had elapsed.

"It's been a pleasure, Mr. Barron," she said, standing, extending her hand.

"May I buy you dinner tonight?" he asked, taking her hand and feeling the warmth of its touch. It was damp and he knew she was as nervous as he was.

"It isn't necessary. I've already given you a substantial order."

"My invitation has nothing to do with your order. You can have it back if you want...the dinner invitation still holds." He hadn't let go of her hand and he felt her demeanor waiver.

"I'm at the Biltmore...seven in the Dining Room." She nodded to Liz and left. The showroom gasped as if a vacuum had left and bursts of air had flooded in.

"That was amazing," Liz said, hanging up garments, and straightening out the showroom, dazed at what had happened. "I felt like I was watching two panthers toy with one another."

"That's a helluva woman," Charlie said, going to a sideboard and pouring himself a drink. "I'll bet she'd eat her young if they'd let her."

Sharon entered the Biltmore's large dining room to the stares of every man in range. One waiter dropped a tray of glasses as he watched her walk by. She was wearing a stunning Givenchy dress, in burgundy, with cutouts at the waist. At the Mart she had been wearing a conservative business suit, little make-up, and serious glasses. The transformation was amazing and Charlie stood to meet her while she was still half way across the room.

"Sharon," he said, smiling lasciviously, but trying not to be too apparent.

"Mr. Barron."

"Please, call me Charlie. You do know how to make an entrance. You are a presence."

"Thank you. A martini, up, Bombay gin, very dry" she said to the hovering waiter.

"I'll have the same."

"I love this room," she said, hoping to break the stare from her date. "It has so much history."

"I'm sorry but I'm trying to connect the woman I battled with all afternoon with the glamorous woman who deigned to have dinner with me this evening."

"That was my combat alter-ego. It wasn't too successful with you but you must admit it was fun."

"If that was fun you must enjoy pulling the wings off of butterflies," he laughed. "No, you're right...it was a challenge. I've never met anyone quite like you."

"Nor I, you," she said as their drinks arrived and they sipped quietly.

Neither asked the other whether they were married, had children, or what astrological sign they were. They actually conversed very little...they were both comfortable with the silence. They enjoyed their dinner, shunned dessert and coffee.

Charlie paid the bill and stood as she waited for him to pull out her chair. Without words he followed her through the lobby and up the elevator to her room. She gave him the key to unlock the door.

He kissed her ardently just as the door clicked shut behind them. She hadn't bothered to turn the lights on as they embraced hungrily in the dark. Their clothes dropped one by one in the entranceway as they slowly made their way into the bedroom.

"Your breasts are beautiful," he said, cupping one in his hand as his tongue began making circles.

"Shhh, don' talk."

She let her fingers play between his legs, purposely avoiding his penis, playing with him. He tried to enter her but she stopped him.

"Patience!"

Now she stroked him gently, her soft fingers touching ever so lightly, sliding up and down. Charlie gasped. He was used to being in control but this was special...very special. Then she guided him in and he was transported.

Sharon climaxed just moments before he did and then she climaxed again, her back arching, gasping, her eyes shut tight. They lay there together, the drapes open, the evening's lights from Pershing Square below illuminating the room.

"You have to leave now," she said so softly he wasn't sure he'd really heard her.

"Why? We can have breakfast in the morning and do this again."

"I like you, Charlie, but I have my own rules. Please don't ask me to explain them.

"Will I see you again?"

"Yes, but I don't know when."

"Then, thank you for a lovely evening," he said, standing at the side of the bed, putting on his shoes. He started to bend down and kiss her but she had already turned away from him. He could tell she was still awake. He stood there for a moment, confused. He closed the door behind him.

"Liz, Charlie here," he said the next day, calling over to the showroom. "What do you know about Sharon Morsey? Yes, I know she's the buyer for Fashion Conspiracy...remember," he said, trying to keep his patience. "I was there with you for three hours. I mean what else do you know...where did she come from...is she married...things like that?   Do some checking for me, please, and call me back when you know something. Yes, it was a great order...you did a terrific job," he said, hanging up, from the young, sweet, but terribly, naïve girl.

"Hi Ruby," Charlie said, reaching his wife at her parent's home in Memphis. "I miss you. How are your parents?"

"Charlie, they don't expect my father to live through the night.   Can you come, please?   This is all pretty overwhelming and between the family, the kids, and losing my father, I'm terribly afraid that I'll lose it."

"I'll be on the next plane."

George Taylor passed that night and his wife, daughter, and son grieved.   Charlie had arrived too late to say goodbye but he didn't care.   George Taylor was a relic from another century.

Katie walked confidently, holding her younger brother's hand as they climbed the steps into the church.   The children were beginning to form their own personalities. The funeral service was a solemn ceremony filled with hosannas now that George was in the lap of Jesus.

Charlie supposed that all the ritual bible-thumping comforted Myrna, but it was the same claptrap he had denounced when his own father had died and the synagogue joined the Rabbi in reading Kaddish, the Jewish prayer for the dead.

Before the service ended, Roger had become restless. It was a wonderful excuse for Charlie to take him outside while Katie joined her mother. Thank you, Roger, he said, silently.

"Henry is going to move his family in with my mother. It will give her company and help them all out financially. I thought I'd stay until he makes the move so she won't be alone. Is that alright?"

"Sure, but I've got to leave. I spent two hours on the phone today with the factory. There isn't anyone to make decisions if I'm not there."

"I understand. I'll get you to the airport. If you fly through St. Louis, you won't need to fly through Dallas."

She gave him a strange look as she said it and for a brief moment he was nonplussed...what did she really mean? Did she know about Ginnie? He certainly couldn't ask.

"Sure...good idea."

He was sitting in the St. Louis airport the next day, waiting for his connecting flight when he made a last minute decision to change his destination from Los Angeles to San Diego after noticing that both flights departed about the same time from adjoining gates. He hoped the coincidence meant something.

Flying into San Diego is a beautiful sight to behold on a clear day...the harbor with an array of naval ships, the iconic Coronado Hotel, Point Loma, and the palm trees of a town that had not yet become a city.

Fashion Conspiracy was in a building off Mission Bay not far away.

"Hello," Charlie said, calling from a phone booth at the airport. "I'd like to speak to Miss Morsey, please. Yes, tell her this is Mr. Charles Barron of Starlet Fashions."

Sharon's extension buzzed four times with no one picking up.

"I'm sorry, she's not answering. She may be out to lunch," the Operator said.

"I don't have an appointment. I just flew in. Does she have a favorite place for lunch? You can tell me...I promise I'm not a stalker."

The Operator laughed. "I'm not sure, but you can try Anthony's Pier One, everyone around here knows it."

Charlie put his suitcase into a locker and walked outside into a warm day and over to a line of waiting taxis.

Anthony's was a favorite local attraction...fresh seafood, ample drinks, and a wonderful location right on the water. Charlie didn't see Sharon at first and he was uncomfortable walking up and down aisles checking out the faces of people eating. He took a seat at the bar, ordered a drink and scanned the luncheon crowd.

Then...there she was...a chameleon with a third look...neither severe nor glamorous but...what was it? Something kept him from rushing over to her. She was sitting with another woman, also attractive, maybe a few years younger, but their body language said it wasn't a business meeting. He watched for several minutes trying to decide whether to go over. Then he thought, 'what the hell,' gulped down his drink and sauntered over.

"Sharon, how nice to see you," he said innocently, holding his empty glass and standing at the edge of their table.

"Charlie!" She was clearly taken aback. "What are you doing here?"

"I just flew in from Memphis. Aren't you going to introduce me to your friend?"

The 'friend' was staring at him icily.

"Of course!" she said, nonplussed. "Eileen Lapin...Charles Barron. Eileen owns several gyms and day spas between La Jolla and San Diego. Charlie owns a large apparel company in Los Angeles, Starlet Fashions."

"May I join you?" he asked, trying to keep his voice innocent, remembering the torrid night he and Sharon had spent and the mysterious way she ended it so abruptly.

Eileen continued to exude a lack of friendliness and he could see her give Sharon a slight nudge below the table.

"Not a good time, Charlie," Sharon said. "We can talk about business another time. Eileen and I need to continue a private conversation."

"Of course. I understand. Eileen, nice to meet you. Sharon, we'll talk soon."

"Charlie, this is Sharon," she said, calling from San Diego a few days later. "Are you free this weekend...we need to talk? I can drive up Saturday morning. Can you meet me in La Jolla? Good, the Surfrider Hotel on Pacific Coast Highway."

The conversation was brief and noncommittal. Charlie tried to analyze what he knew, what he suspected, and what was missing. Maybe he'd learn more this weekend.

Charlie had been scheduled to fly to New York and his mind told him he should...but he couldn't. He needed to sort out this situation with Sharon. He forgot New York and drove to La Jolla. He left his Encino home nice and early. It got him to La Jolla in less than two hours, breaking more than one speeding law. He changed into his trunks and sat at the pool sipping a Bloody Mary. He'd left a note in the room for Sharon to join him.

An hour later she arrived wearing a one-piece Jantzen swimsuit in bright red. He'd seen the same suit in magazine ads but none of them did justice to that swimsuit the way Sharon did.

"Let's go back to the room," Charlie suggested. "I like getting a tan...I hate looking like a boiled lobster."

Once in the room he showered. When he came out wearing a hotel robe, Sharon was sitting on the patio watching the ocean.

"You look deep in thought," Charlie said, rubbing her neck. "Anything I can do to make you more relaxed?"

"I owe you an explanation."

"You really don't. I'm just happy you're here with me."

"Eileen is my girlfriend. We've been together on and off for longer than I can remember. She was married once. She even had an abortion but the marriage never made sense to her. She found me when I was down. I'd gone through three relationships with men that didn't work. I liked men…at least I thought I did, but the relationships always seemed to get so complicated. With Eileen it isn't complicated."

"OK…I'm happy for you. Then why are you here?"

"Because something happened in that showroom that I couldn't explain. It unraveled everything that had begun to make sense."

"I'm sorry I unsettled your life but you need to know that you unsettled my life as well."

"Anyway, I was trying to forget you and go on with Eileen as before but the moment we both saw you at the restaurant, she knew. I'm not sure what she knew but she understood that you had come between us."

"So, where does that leave us?"

"I don't know," Sharon confessed, standing and coming over to Charlie. He held her and she cried, deep sobs, as if everything inside her that had been tied in a neat knot was suddenly coming apart, one strand at a time.

They made love that afternoon…and that evening, and again the next morning. The hotel brought them food from a nearby restaurant. Mostly they sat together, facing the beach and holding one another.

"Sharon, we both have obligations. You have Eileen and I have a wife and two young children but one thing I know...we're meant to be together. What you do when you're with Eileen is your business and I would never judge. I've been with other women since Ruby and I married but they've been one night stands...it was the sex. This is different. I don't know if it's love...it may be, but we need to be together until we both find out."

Ruby had tried to reach Charlie several times at the office and at home to tell him she was on her way and what time the plane would land. The office didn't know where he was. They thought he might have left early for New York. Could something have happened to him, she wondered. My God, he might be lying in a hospital somewhere...even the morgue. When she couldn't get answers she could only think the worse. This wasn't like him...not like him at all.

Ruby landed back in Los Angeles and took a taxi from the airport. It was so expensive she barely had an extra dollar for a tip. The children slept all the way home and everything was locked up when she arrived early afternoon on Sunday. She got the children sorted out before she sat down, nervous and on the verge of tears.

Charlie pulled into the driveway in the middle of the evening, intending to take a shower and repack for an early morning flight to New York. Somewhere on the drive home he realized he hadn't checked in with Ruby all weekend.   She's probably busy with her parents, he rationalized.

The children were asleep as Charlie opened the door and found his wife sitting quietly, holding a drink. It wasn't her first that evening.

"Ruby, my God...I didn't expect you home.   What happened? Is everything alright? Are the kids OK?" he chattered, not knowing what to say but sensing that things might be fine as long as he didn't stop talking.

Ruby gave into her first reaction and threw her glass across the room at him.

"You son-of-a-bitch. I've been worrying about you all weekend. I couldn't reach you from Memphis and when I changed planes I tried again. When I landed you still were unavailable.   No one knew where Charles Barron had disappeared to and now you arrive home at the end of a weekend with a face that says it got too much sun this weekend."

"Listen," he said, forming his thoughts at atomic speed, "I needed to get away by myself and this seemed as good a time as any. I'm sorry I didn't check in but I didn't want to talk to anyone. There are things going on regarding Starlet that I haven't shared with you and it was a chance to think things through. I went down the coast on the spur of the moment...checked into a hotel and spent the weekend sitting by a pool and tried to resolve some things. That's all...nothing more."

Ruby looked at her husband...the man she'd married. The man with whom she bore two children...the man whose bed she shared...but who else did he share a bed with when he was away from home? It would be so easy to believe him.

"Charlie, I'm drained...my parents, the long trip home with the children, and your absence. Maybe I've had too much to drink and I'm not thinking clearly. I'm glad you're safe. I'm going to sleep," she said walking by him and shutting the door to their bedroom.

He blinked as the door closed, not knowing whether she believed him. He still loved Ruby and the domestic life that made him feel normal...upper middle class and successful...definitely normal. But what about Sharon?

Sharon is a fire I can't quench. Can I love two women at the same time? What the fuck have I gotten myself into he wondered as he cleaned up the spill from the thrown glass and fixed himself a fresh drink.

He postponed his morning departure, hoping to smooth things over with Ruby and spend some time with the children but except for a few words, Ruby had dressed and been out the door, driving the children to school. He ordered two dozen roses to be delivered to the house that afternoon, left a note professing his love, and drove to the airport.

The next two weeks passed quickly. Starlet's line was exciting and three showroom sales people kept busy writing orders while Charlie worked to keep each contact with each customer personal. He called Ruby every evening dutifully but her comments were perfunctory and emotionless. He'd also spoken to Sharon at work. She was not about to interrupt her evenings with Eileen until she understood her own feelings.

"Charlie, we've got a problem!"   Ken Miller, Starlet's Sales Manager, said, walking into his office and collapsing into one of the overstuffed chairs. I think you should call in Bunny, Papa and Sam."

Charlie would have preferred to decide who heard what but there was something in Ken's tone…usually calm and unflappable that kept him from interrupting.

"Last week I had an order cancelled by K-Mart. They mentioned something about being able to get the same tops somewhere else for less. Those guys are always pretty price sensitive so I didn't think much of it. Now, in the past two days, Penney's and Sears have also cancelled their orders.

"That was way too much coincidence so I called my closest contact at each chain. It seems the sales rep from California Cooking came in offering the identical style, identical fabric and colors at $1 to $2 less per garment."

"It can't be the same," Bunny said as Sam and Papa both began speaking over one another while Charlie sat silently, understanding immediately what was taking place.

"Will Duval," he muttered to himself, as he picked up the phone. "Neil…Charlie! I need you to come over. Thanks."

"You need us to check everyone who works here when they leave?" Papa asked. "I can do that."

"I'm not sure. I know where the information is going. I just don't know who's taking it out of here."

"Probably not one of our sewing contractors," Sam Martinez added. "They get the goods too late in the production cycle. Someone is getting the information earlier."

"The sample room...or the design room," Bunny said. "Someone involved in making my samples. But I've known them all a long time, all three of them."

"Who are they?" Charlie asked.

"Luisa Ortega, Ann Cho and Sylvia Mantena."

"Let's leave out Cho for the moment. Tell me about Luisa and Sylvia," Charlie said, focusing in on the problem. "Meanwhile, Bunny, you stay. You three can leave...and Ken, thanks. I'll get this sorted out and please, keep this to yourselves. We can't solve it if everyone in the company knows about it."

A few moments later Neil Pastore arrived, threw his cape on the chair and sat down. Charlie motioned Bunny to close the door while Charlie filled his partner in on what was happening.

"The rumor is that Will Duval is now tied in with mobsters from Vegas instead of New York. And, I suspect that he's beginning to run scared. What he's doing is pretty high risk. He's never been able to come up with a line as good as ours so he uses other tactics...strong arming buyers or, this time, stealing our designs. It's touchy," Charlie continued.   "If it wasn't for the mob connection..."

"Say no more," Neil interrupted.   "Bunny, get me everything you've got on the fabrics he's stealing and you all go back to running Starlet...and, Charlie...continue to produce their orders."

Charlie had learned enough through the years to not ask too many questions.   There was an underside to the apparel business that was safer to avoid.

Four weeks later the goods were ready to ship and the warehouse was stuffed.   Neither Neil nor the customers had been in contact and Charlie was beginning to wonder who he could call to buy all the unsold tops overflowing the building.

"Charlie, you'll never guess what happened?" Ken shouted into the phone. "Penney's just called. Their rep from California Cooking called. He's asking for a three week extension and permission to substitute a different fabric. The buyer was royally pissed...he'd gone out on a limb when he was told he could get the identical garment for less money.

"And when I told his boss, their Merchandising Vice President, we never stopped production on their order, he screamed and offered to come over and give me an immediate blow job. I told him he wasn't my type but to get us the shipping information...the goods were ready to go."

"Amazing...and Sears and Kmart?"

"I've got calls into them. They said they'd get back to me before the end of the day. What the fuck did your partner do?"

"I have some ideas but I don't intend to ask," Charlie said, fully knowing that Neil had used his connections with the fabric mills to keep Duval from getting his fabric orders filled.

Will's Las Vegas partners weren't happy. They didn't know, and probably wouldn't have cared, about cancelled orders or Duval's gimmicks to build his sales. What they did care about was information from Fred Stanton that their operating partner was a little more than light-fingered in selling off inventory for cash and lavish expenses. With sales of the company flat, the shortfall appeared as bright as Vegas neon.

And Will Duval...he was toast. They roughed him up pretty badly but they didn't kill him. They did take every dollar they could find and with the threat that they'd break his fingers...one at a time, slowly, until he finally confessed to the location of a safety deposit box he had kept secret.

"Charlie...phone call. He wouldn't give his name," the receptionist said.

"This is Charlie Barron. Who is this?"

"Hello Charlie. Will Duval! I'm sure you remember your old friend."

"Of course, Will. How're things at California Cooking?"

"You know fucking-a-well how things are. Don't play the innocent with me. Clever shit with the fabric but don't turn your back or walk down any dark alleys, Charlie. I'm not gone from your life...not now...not ever."

He broke the connection and Charlie sat for a long moment listening to the dial tone.

eleven

Broadway Limited

"I think we need to separate for a while," Ruby said. "Whatever is going on in the rest of your life is destroying our family. Katie and Roger are both acting up in school and at home they're impossible to handle.   Maybe it's me …I don't know. I'm just not good being both mother and father."

"I don't know what's going on either. You've had the children in Memphis away from their normal routine and now you want me out of their lives. Are you sure you're thinking clearly?"

"Probably not.   All I know is that you are involved with another woman…maybe more than one given your history. I want to know her name and what you intend to do. I know you weren't alone that weekend. You don't lie well…you're very transparent."

"Her name is Sharon and I am completely muddled as to my feelings. I love you and our children and our life. I may also be in love with her…I don't know," he confessed, glad to finally verbalize his confusion, wherever the truth took him.

Ruby collapsed into a seat, tears rolling down her cheek.

It was one thing to throw out an accusation but entirely another to learn that it was true. There had always been that tiny hope that Charlie's denials were the truth.

"Daddy, when are you coming back?" Katie asked him as he struggled to explain to his daughter that he'd be continue to see her but he wouldn't be living at home.

"I don't want you to leave." Tears were beginning to form and slide down her cheeks. Roger refused to cry but he stood nearby, his teeth clenched.

"Listen, kids," Charlie said, bending down. "Sometimes Mommies and Daddies need time away from one another. That doesn't mean either of us love you less. I'll still see you. How about I take you both to the zoo this Sunday? You can get some cotton candy...I know you'd like that."

"Can we get pancakes first? We can go to Du Par's at the Farmer's Market...can we?" she bargained.

"Sure, if it's OK with your mother," he surrendered, looking at Ruby standing off to one side. She nodded, her eyes red as well.

"You're more than welcome to come with us," he said to her.

"I'll see."

Charlie checked into the Biltmore Hotel where he and Sharon had enjoyed their first dinner and their first night together. He could still see her Givenchy dress. He got hard as he remembered unzipping it as the door to the room clicked behind him.

It was easy for Sharon to be in Los Angeles during the week. She needed to work with an array of the local apparel manufacturers. Weekends were more difficult. Those days belonged to Eileen.

For the next few weeks Charlie and Sharon spent evenings and mornings together. Hungrily they also spent their nights. Sharon seemed to finally be able to smile. Their sex was fun and Charlie discovered he really didn't need coke to get a high when he was with her. There was a sadness when they parted from one another Friday mornings. They lingered over breakfast and a pall fell over their room as she packed her small suitcase.

"See you Monday evening," he said.

"Until Monday," she responded, kissing him, wanting to say more but not knowing what words to use.

Most of Charlie's weekends were set aside for his children, Katie and Roger, unless he was at Market Week in New York or Dallas. He tried to leave those for his sales people but the customers expected to see him and orders were always smaller when he stayed in Los Angeles.

Charlie would pick up the children after school on Friday and return them to Encino on Sunday close to dinner time. Most Sundays Ruby had dinner waiting for them and invited Charlie to share it with them. He did. It gave them a few hours to talk after the children were bathed and tucked into bed.

Well into the second month it was clear there had been no resolution of their dilemma.

"You know, we can't continue like this forever," Ruby said. "I think it's time I filed for a divorce."

The words were like a knife to his heart. Sharon was pressing him as well although she didn't seem ready to give up Eileen either.

"Charlie, we are messing up the lives of people we care about and I don't know what to do," Sharon said. They had walked across the street and were sitting in Pershing Square watching people scurrying every which way.

"Eileen and I have discussed it. I'm going to take a two month leave of absence. She and I are going to disappear together to some island. I love you, Charlie. You've restored my feelings about men...you have, but I can't surrender the feelings I have for Eileen. Please tell me you understand."

"How can I argue about intense feelings for a woman? Those are the only feelings I've ever had. I've just never had to compete with a woman for another woman's affections. Sharon, I love you. I've also found out I need you. Ruby is happy to give me a divorce. Why don't you and I run away to Las Vegas and get married as soon as the divorce is final? Eileen can't love you as much as I do. We just feel right in one another's arms."

"It is so tempting to just surrender. I feel so safe when we're together but it wouldn't be fair to everything Eileen and I feel for one another. Charlie, I'm just mixed-up. I've never really been mixed up about anything in my entire life, but I can't resolve this so easily. I love you both too much. Will you give me two months...please?"

He nodded, feeling his insides knot up.

Sharon kissed him, stood up from the bench, and returned to the hotel to get her things. When she drove off an hour later, he was still sitting there. He looked so lonely she wanted to stop and take him in her arms. She didn't.

Charlie rented a two-bedroom apartment in Malibu. He could drop over Topanga Canyon and pick up the children in a short time. He never made the trip, however, without looking to see if Jessica was there, perhaps shopping. He wasn't sure where she was. She could be bathing in that filthy river in India with all the cows and burned dead people. Why would someone want to do that? Wherever she is, I hope she's happy.

What is it about me, he wondered. Both his wives, Jessica and Ruby, had left him. He'd also lost Sharon. His score card was zero for three. He knew he hadn't been a faithful mate but they'd all known that when they met him. But he loved them...really loved them. Anything else was just sex...fucking around. They were all relationships that meant nothing. Damn women...too complicated. With that thought, he gunned the car and bolted forward, nearly sideswiping an 18-wheeler.

At least Starlet was doing well. It was now an established company with its own mini-departments in several of the majors. It was the only thing in his life that seemed to keep him going...maybe that and his two children would be enough for a while.

He didn't have financial worries, either. He could ski when he wanted and fuck whoever he wanted to. He missed domestic life but, in truth, it had its drawbacks for someone like him. He still enjoyed 'blow' when he was at a party but he could function without it if he had to. Neil Pastore was still a prick and Charlie had given up trying to become a full 50% partner...too expensive.

He knew it all couldn't last. He wasn't sure how or where, but he knew he'd succeed in messing things up...it was all going too well.

Neil Pastore invited him to come to his office Wednesday at 2:00 P.M. It was two days after Charlie had returned from showing a small holiday line in New York. Neil's invitation was very unusual...it was a very specific invitation at a very specific time. Charlie arrived several minutes late, on purpose...he hated feeling that he had been summoned to the Principal's office.

Neil scowled at his partner's tardiness. He knew it had been intentional. The two men who had been sitting on the couch stood when Charlie entered.

"Charlie, these men are from Broadway, Limited. This is Harvey Thompson and his Chief Finance Officer, Bud Cob. They're in from New York for this meeting. Gentlemen, my tardy partner, Charles Barron."

"I'm sorry I'm late. Target stores is interested in doing business and it was a rather prolonged telephone conversation."

"Business first," Harvey Thompson said, smiling, and making every effort to be charming. He was well over 6'4" and trim. His green eyes glistened when he spoke. He had started Broadway, Limited fifteen years ago. He concentrated on off-price merchandise...buying garments manufacturers couldn't sell...overproduction, cancelled orders.

Harvey had opened his first store in Harlem, the second in Greenwich Village, and never stopped. Bud Cob joined him a few years later and together they began buying companies. Harvey Thompson's life was displayed in Forbes and Business Week...an American success story.

"And we are all here why?" Charlie asked, sitting himself down and wondering what the hell was going on.

"Broadway, Limited wants to buy Starlet Fashions."

"And why would we want to sell when we've almost doubled sales every year?"

"Because they've offered us a terrific price and they have the contacts and distribution to take Starlet to a hundred million."

"Sorry, gentlemen, you are here on a fool's errand. I have no desire to be a small fish in your big pond."

"Charlie, I don't think you understand," Neil said, a deep frown furrowing across his forehead. "I've already signed the contract. I own 60% of Starlet...I didn't need your approval. It's a done deal and you are going to be a rich man."

"Neil," Charlie said, standing and walking over to pour himself a drink. "You were a mother-fucker when we started this business and you are still a mother-fucker. We could have reached a hundred million on our own...we didn't need a leaky umbrella and Broadway is a leaky umbrella. Their sales have hit a plateau...they need us more than we need them."

"Not exactly true," Bud Cob interjected. "We just had two difficult quarters."

"Bud, may I call you Bud? No offense, but that is a crock of shit...a very biased interpretation of your company's current situation. Neil, you should have asked me, and if you'd cared at all about the Starlet we built, you would have.

"Broadway, Limited is like Montgomery Ward, a monster retail chain that operated a half century ago...lots of cash and no market...no customers. But...fuck it...it's a done deal. You got yours." Charlie stood and headed for the door.

"Please don't leave Mr. Barron. You are part of the package. We want you to continue to run Starlet. We don't plan on making any changes in your operation."

"And, why would I? The only change is that I would have you to deal with instead of Neil. Say," he smiled. "That is an improvement. I'm leaving. Come to Starlet tomorrow morning and we'll talk. Neil, it will be a real fucking pleasure to have you out of my life."

"Good morning, Gentlemen.   Welcome to your new company.   Alice," he shouted...he hated the intercom, "bring us coffee."

Harvey Thompson and Bud Cob smiled, knowing it was important that they put their best foot forward.   They needed to keep the man across from them running the company. They had discussed it last night, surprised that Barron knew so much about their financial condition. Broadway had made two bad investments.

They'd bought two companies last year and now each of them was floundering to survive.   One company had bet their entire season on a Gothic look being popular and when it wasn't, they were saddled with a warehouse filled with black skulls and devils.   The other company was convinced corduroy was set to replace denim.   It didn't. Now Thompson badly needed to acquire a successful asset like Starlet to right their ship and buoy their stock price.

"You've bought a good company," Charlie said, knowing he was in control of a situation foisted on him unexpectedly.   He'd always thought it might be another five years before he'd sell Starlet.   Nothing is forever in this business.

"We're prepared to offer you a sweet package if you'll stay," Harvey Thompson said.   "We have someone ready to step in if you leave but he isn't our first choice."

"Would you mind telling me who it is?"

"I'd prefer not to at this point," Harvey replied.   He wasn't new to this game.   He figured, rightly, that Charlie wanted to know the quality of the man they had in their pocket. He could measure it against his opinion of his own value.

Harvey Thompson was an ex-prize fighter...a middle weight...a good club fighter. He'd won a bronze medal in the Olympics and used it to launch a business career, getting an MBA evenings at NYU.

It was rumored that his first money came from New York's mob family but no one could prove anything. He'd built Broadway, Limited, primarily from acquisitions, centralizing each garment company's production and shipping but letting them control their own design and sales efforts. It worked for a while...then it got stale and, like a Ponzi scheme, they needed to keep buying successful companies to support the belief they were a growth company. Enter Starlet!

"Not important," Charlie said. "Give me a number and I'll tell you yes or no. How does that sound?"

"It isn't one number," Bud Cob said, speaking for the first time. "If you meet all the targets you can easily make a quarter million."

"And if I don't make the targets...what's the minimum guarantee?"

"Your base salary is $60,000 a year."

Charlie laughed. "That's funny...very funny. Gentlemen, enjoy your new company. My answer is no but out of respect to the team I built, I'm willing to stay and help with the changeover at a salary of $10,000.00 per month, a minimum of three months."

"That's an outrageous amount," Cob said, insulted.

"Then don't take it," Charlie smiled. "Frankly, forget it. I'll be out of here tomorrow, if that's acceptable to you. I promise not to steal the ashtrays."

"I think we'd rather have you out today then," Harvey Thompson said. "Bud will remain here until you leave."

"Suit yourself. Alice, get everyone in here…now," he shouted.

Charlie introduced the new owners while Bunny, Papa and some of the others stared, mouths agape.

"You guys have all been wonderful…Starlet wouldn't have made it without your combined talents. And…you're all invited to my place in Malibu for a huge party next Sunday. We'll make it a huge blowout. Alice, pack up my things, please. Perhaps one of you can bring them Sunday." He looked at Harvey Thompson, hoping his voice wouldn't break.

"Take care of them, Harvey. They're a terrific group and they can make you happy you bought Starlet."

Nearly everyone showed up that Sunday. Bunny brought her husband, Papa brought his wife and nearly a hundred people crowded into, over, and around Charlie's Malibu complex thanks to Valets parking cars, an energetic caterer, and tolerant neighbors, who had also been invited.

Everyone had been given a bonus calculated by Audrey Milton according to the job they'd held and how long they'd been with the company. All the bonus money had come from Charlie. Neil Pastore had refused to contribute money or even express his gratitude. He had ended his relationship with Starlet as arrogantly as he'd begun.

"What are you going to do now, Charlie?" Bunny asked. "You know I have no desire to work for anyone else and that's probably true of several of the others as well."

"Tell them all to hang in there. I understand Harvey Thompson is going to stay and oversee things for a while. Either the man he told me he had in the wings turned him down or he never existed. That's their problem, but Starlet is a good company. Me, I'm going to take a month or two and get to know my children again."

Charlie couldn't remember the last time he woke up alone without a clear plan for the day. It was both exhilarating and depressing. The first week was unique. He would take a beach chair and sit at the water's edge, letting the waves touch his legs, reading or napping until some young nubile girl came by and needed his attention.

He could have enjoyed a new one each day during the summer, and often did, careful that an underage Tammy King wasn't among them. Most days he didn't even bother to shave. The girls who walked by and eyed him didn't seem to mind.

Katie and Roger loved the beach. His daughter had entered her teens and it was clear she was going to be a beauty. Roger's voice had dropped as he passed through puberty and discovered girls. Charlie had tried repeatedly to reach Sharon but she'd refused to take his calls. She had stopped coming to Los Angeles as well. The two months she had requested to consider her conundrum had come and gone. He knew Sharon had made her decision, and it wasn't to be him. In a way, he had known it would happen this way.

Ruby had begun to rebuild her life, reaching out to friends, traveling to Tennessee, and exploring what it was like to be a financially comfortable unattached woman in Encino.

But the apparel business was in Charlie's blood and each day he'd read the Apparel News and Women's Wear Daily. He'd flip through the pages of Vogue and Elle. He was taking flying lessons at the Van Nuys airport but he was no good at it. He would overact on turns and hated learning a new language of roll, pitch, and yaw. When he nearly blew a tire by landing too hard, he thanked the instructor and walked away.

The first anniversary of the sale came without celebration but he knew retirement wasn't for him. He had that itch to be in the thick of things again. He began exploring the possibility of going back into business. Did he need a partner? Could he finance the business on his own? Would his team come back and work for him?

Starlet was moving along at a horizontal level...it was neither growing nor was it collapsing. Nearly two years had passed since it became part of Broadway Limited. A few new people had been added...a few had left. Bunny was still the lead designer but as Charlie walked through the racks at Bullock's looking at what was being offered, he could tell that she was stagnant. There was no excitement...nothing that couldn't have been created by a hundred other designers.

twelve

Galaxy Fashions

"Sam, I'm decided to get back into the business," Charlie said. He'd invited both Sam Simon from Manufacturer's Bank and Irwin Ross from Walter Heller Financial to join him for lunch. The three men were sitting at Sing How's, a new Chinese Restaurant that had opened in the Mart. His two guests were enjoying a cocktail. Charlie had opted for Perrier and his abstinence impressed them...he knew it would.

"I'm going to call the new company Galaxy Fashions. I'll be financing the start-up capital myself but, as usual, I'll need your support for credit and factoring."

"Charlie, you know the business is changing," Irwin Ross said. He was 6'5" and overflowed the booth. Heller was a credit giant with offices around the world but Los Angeles was Irwin's private fiefdom. He knew where all the financial bones were buried and who would be out of business next month.

"China is beginning to become more and more of a factor. The Japanese are doing a better job of printing on fabric; the Chinese quotas on cotton are affecting that price, and Mexican labor is moving jobs out of Los Angeles and the rest of the country. Our country is losing garment manufacturing jobs and those that are too small to do import programs are struggling. Did you hear about Phil Banyon...Banyon Apparel?"

"I know Phil," Charlie said. "Not well...we always sold into different departments but he seemed like a nice enough guy.

As I recall he was in business with his wife. She designed, he sold."

"That's the guy," Irwin said. "They caught the damn fool falsifying invoices and sending them to my receivable people to get cash. That's a no-no. An invoice is supposed to guarantee the goods were shipped. His goods were still hanging in the warehouse. Anyway the Feds busted him for wire fraud.

"He's been sentenced to two years in a Federal penitentiary and his wife has to take care of their young daughter by herself. She'll also need to explain to the girl that her father is a convicted felon. It's a sad story but guys who are on the brink are likely to try risky things."

They all took a pause and the silence hung over the table before Sam Simon asked the critical question.

"What makes you think this is the right time to start a company?"

"Sam, it's the right time because you men are sitting here with me. This country will always have a fashion industry regardless of where the crap is manufactured. We have more than two hundred million people who want to look prettier than the person sitting next to them ...prettier, different...and at a better price.

"That's what I've always done. I know how to do it...you know I do. I've done it before and I'm going to do it again. So, what do you say? Will you toast to Galaxy Fashions with me?"

Irwin and Sam looked at one another. They both liked Charlie Barron but they also had a lot of hesitation. He was like a meteor that could burn up and crash.

"How about finding a partner...maybe someone who could handle production the way you did the first time?" Sam asked, not totally convinced.

"You remember how that turned out?" Charlie reminded him. "Pablo was a closet gay and that damned revolution in El Salvador messed up an entire season. Maybe I should try Neil Pastore again? I understand he took his money and left the business."

"You can say it was a smart thing for him to do. You made the man a lot of money. What's the real reason you want to do this...I'm sure it isn't the money?"

"I hate retirement...I need the energy of building a company...it's what makes me tick. Look, if you know someone who meshes with my vision of what I want Galaxy to be, I'll consider it, but I don't want to wait while we start searching. Let me get started. If you find someone we can talk about it. Meanwhile, are we a go? "

"Charlie, you are still full of crap," Sam laughed, raising his glass, "but I gotta' love you. We're with you."

Irwin nodded.

Charlie Barron knew he was being brash and overconfident but he didn't know how to move forward any other way. Starting a company was going to take every bit of cash in the bank and every bit of green he'd stashed away through the years. It took a hell of a lot more to start a company in the 1980's than it did in the 1950's and '60's.

Broadway, Limited was still pushing the Starlet label but, where Charlie had it in better stores like Macy's and Dillard's, it had lost its panache and moved down the food chain. It was now selling at K-Mart and J C Penney's.

Bunny had stuck it out with the new owners, afraid to face working for some asshole. The industry was filled with them. She wasn't happy but it was a job. Her biggest frustration was that the Starlet sales people had a complete lack of imagination when it came to styling.

"We want basics," they said every season. "Nothing too flashy."

So she gave them uninspired basics. And then Charlie let her know he was ready to go to work again. It took her only minutes to gather her things and walk out of Starlet's building. She hadn't even asked her old boss if he was going to pay her a salary. She was ready to join him under any terms.

"I want 5% of the business," she said, sitting across from his half-furnished office in a small complex off Alameda Street.

"Oh, you do?" he laughed. "I would have given you 10% but you're a tough negotiator so we'll settle on 5%. I'm glad we're together again."

"So am I...but I also need a refrigerator stocked with my Coca-Cola and no comments about my smoking."

"Agreed!"

Charlie signed a lease on a showroom at the Apparel Mart, across from the bank, and in the center of Los Angeles' fashion hub. He hired a showroom girl to keep an eye on things and arrange appointments. For now, until he could hire a quality sales rep, he'd personally handle all the accounts.

But New York was critical to Galaxy's success. He arranged to share a showroom in the 1411 building in New York and hired Adrienne, a dark-haired beauty from Milan, who spoke with her hands in constant motion. Her English was a polyglot mixed with Italian but no one cared.

The male buyers and merchandisers were entranced and ordered whatever styles she recommended. The women stared at her beauty and the creative ensembles she wore, convinced this girl had an instinctive awareness of what would sell in their store. The men just stared.

"Papa," he said, sipping an ice tea, and sitting across from his old shipping manager at Joe K's in Vernon and enjoying a hot corned beef sandwich stacked high. "You've got a little more grey in your hair these days."

"You haven't gotten any younger either," Abel Edwards laughed. He had gained some weight...his hairline had receded slightly but the glint in his eyes was still there. He was glad to see his old boss. He knew about all the shit Charlie Barron had pulled with his old partner but the man sitting across from him had always treated him respectfully.

And Papa hadn't always been lucky enough to say that. Where he worked...if anything went wrong...check the big black dude. Starlet had been different. Crazy Bunny always came back to chat and have a cigarette and Charlie always gave him a 'high 5.'

"Want to come back and work with me? Bunny is designing and I'd sure love to have you run the shipping department."

"Charlie, I've got grandkids now and a wife who likes the stability of a weekly check. Every time I think about you it's like a 4th of July celebration...could be a rocket that lights up the sky or a dud."

"This is going to be a rocket, Papa...an honest-to-God rocket! C'mon...it'll be fun."

"Are you going to explain to my wife the first time I don't get paid?"

"No, I think I'd let you do that," he laughed.

"Who's going to be running production?"

"I don't know yet. Any suggestions?"

"Most of the ones I know you know, coke addicts, kickback artists, scammers. This town is full of them and it's easy for them to make all kinds of extra money if they're so inclined."

"That's true of shipping managers as well but you never did. At least I don't think you did."

"I didn't," Papa said. "I like to look in the mirror each morning and know that when I'm telling my kids how to do things right...not lie or steal or cheat, that I'm not bullshitting them."

Charlie smiled. Abel Edwards was a good man...someone you definitely wanted on your team.

But Papa was right. Finding a Production Manager was more difficult. Each man he interviewed was either unqualified, overpaid, or a slug.

"I may have found our Production Manager," Papa said, nearly a month later. He'd had to argue with his wife to join Charlie but she saw the fun in her husband's eyes whenever he talked about crazy Charlie Barron. She gave him an OK and got a kiss and a hug that convinced her it was the right decision.

"What's his name?"

"It isn't a he...it's a she, Liliana Espinoza. Everyone calls her Lili. She's been a broker for the last few years, placing garments for small companies that can't afford their own production person."

"A she? A woman running production? I don't think so. She wouldn't have the balls to get the best price or hound a contractor for better delivery. Let's keep looking."

"Charlie, you are the boss but you need to talk to this lady. I don't think she's afraid of a thing."

"Miss Espinoza...please, come in," Charlie said a few days later. Liliana Espinoza was the only girl in a family with four older brothers and a father who was a drunk and liked to molest his daughter.

One night when Liliana was twelve, the brothers had had enough. They interrupted their father's drunken activity. They picked him up bodily and threw him out of the house, threatening to kill him if they ever saw him again...they never did. They taught their tiny, innocent, sister how to fight. She never stopped.

The entire family had come across the border together ten years earlier, scaling the fence across from Tijuana, ignoring the hoots and warnings of the Coyotes.

"Without us you will be caught," they catcalled. The Yankee immigration officers will like your sister...muy dulce."

The Espinoza family still functioned as a unit although two of the brothers were married. The men had all inveigled themselves into the Teamsters Union but they insisted that Lili graduate from high school. She did, and two years of college after that.

"Thank you, but you can call me Lili," she said, finding a seat opposite the big desk. Her feet needed to be on their toes for them to touch the floor.

"You're pretty tiny for a Production Manager."

"I'm big enough.   If you've got garments you want made, I'll get them made, to spec, and on time."

"Lili, you have a good reputation but what I see in front of me is a pretty young thing that someone will scoop up in their pocket and have for dessert."

"Then you aren't looking at this the right way. I have a black belt in judo and the last guy that thought he wanted to try a Mexican dessert ended up in the Emergency Room. If you want the job done, hire me. If not, let me leave...I have better things to do than chat with a good looking guy with his own fancy reputation."

"You'd be a real bitch to work with, wouldn't you?" Charlie laughed, not sure whether he wanted to hassle every day with someone so confrontational. "Why'd you leave your last job?   I don't see any sort of letter of recommendation with your resume?"

"No, you won't. The two owners are awaiting sentence on Federal drug charges. You know the Dickson kids...they had this street wear line and they asked me to do production. I turned them down for months but they're cute and persistent so I joined them. But it never felt quite right. Whenever I came up front to their offices, they'd stuff things in drawers.

"One day I arrived about the same time as a small army of DEA agents, complete with weapons and Kevlar vests. It seems the Dickson kids were using the garment business as a front for their more lucrative heroin business. The agents questioned me for hours before letting me go. No final check, no severance package, and definitely no letter of recommendation."

"Their father was a shmuck also. Not surprising about the kids. OK...you've got the job."

"Get me fabric on time and expect reasonable production schedules...then I'm an absolute lamb. I only bite when I get fucked over."

"Well, we've got that in common, at least. Are you married? Want to go for a drink and celebrate our new union?"

"I'm married. My husband is 6'4", 230 lbs. and a police officer in Hawthorne. He's also very jealous so you may want to rethink your drink and celebration offer."

"Understood. I'll see you Monday."

Lili stood and smiled, "Monday."

"OK, Papa, we've got ourselves a Production Manager. I hired your friend, Lili. You never mentioned she was married."

"Married? She's not married," Papa laughed.

Charlie had to pause and realize he'd been had. "That's a funny lady...a very funny lady."

thirteen

Harvey Thompson

Harvey Thompson was not a person who liked to lose money and he'd been sloppy in buying Starlet. It was insane to complete a deal without making certain that its key player would remain part of the team. Now, nearly four years later the company was still flat, and at a level half of what they were doing when he'd purchased it. He'd tried hiring different sales people, different production people, and even threatened to fire the damned designer. Nothing worked and he needed to resolve it sooner rather than later.

He definitely needed some time away from the problem. He decided to leave Los Angeles and return to New York but take a detour by spending a weekend in Las Vegas. He loved Vegas and while any of several hotels were willing to roll out the red carpet for a high-roller, he preferred staying in the tower at Caesar's Palace.

When he checked in he found a note inviting him to meet with a particular man in the lobby bar. There was no name. He didn't need to worry, it said...the man would recognize him and expected to see him there at 9:00 PM that evening.

Harvey came down from his room around 7:00 and sat

down at a $25 Blackjack table. It was still early and he was able to play alone. He preferred it that way. He was down several hundred dollars and getting into a foul mood when he won four hands in a row and recouped nearly half his losses. At 9:00 he tipped the dealer a green chip and walked over to the lobby bar.

Before he could order a drink a small, well-dressed man approached and sat down unannounced.

"Jack Daniels, neat," the man said, nodding to Harvey to order whatever he liked. The man wasn't threatening but he had an intensity that somehow seemed worse.

"I like mysteries as well as anyone, but isn't this a little film noir?" Harvey said after the cocktail waitress left, trying to sound casual as he sized up this stranger.

"My people own a woman's sportswear company in Los Angeles called California Cooking. We don't want to own it anymore and we want Broadway Limited to buy it from us."

"Listen, whoever you are. I'm sure your *'people'* can drop me somewhere in the desert and let my bones dry up, if you choose, but this is not the way to do business. Introduce me to your boss and let's discuss it professionally."

"I'm authorized to finalize any reasonable arrangement."

"I know California Cooking. It had a nice run and then it tanked. Maybe it was the rumor that it was just a front for one or two of the local casinos."

"I can't say.   The men who arranged the original purchase are all dead...rest their souls, and our need for that outlet has gone away. What I can tell you is that you can buy it at a good price. We want out and we'd rather not just shut it down."

"Why not?" Harvey asked.

"People are less inclined to look too close at the records if a business continues."

"Look, I've already got one company in that same market."

"And it ain't doin' shit," the man said, his voice taking on a more determined tone. "Maybe if you merge the two companies something stronger might come out of it."

"Putting two turds together doesn't make it smell better," Harvey said, knowing his options were going to be very limited.

Three weeks later the California Apparel News released printed an important story:

> *Harvey Thompson, Chief Executive Officer of Broadway Limited, announced today that his company had purchased the assets of California Cooking, a Southern California woman's sportswear manufacturer, for an undisclosed amount of money.*
>
> *"Our two companies have decided that it is in the best interest of both companies to join forces. Design*

and sales will remain separate but being able to combine production, shipping, and finance, will save a great deal of money and allow us to better compete with the flood of cheap imports being thrown at the nation's retailers. We intend to have creative designs, manufactured in the Unites States, at competitive prices. We will be announcing a new Chief Operating Officer in the next few weeks who shares our vision."

Charlie read the article and smiled. All he could think about was the old saw, 'whatever goes around, comes around.' He didn't realize how right he was. Another announcement, a month later, in much smaller type, proclaimed Will Duval, new President of Starlet – California, a wholly owned subsidiary of Broadway Limited. That was a surprise he hadn't anticipated.

Will Duval had left Los Angeles surprised that his ass was still intact. It could have turned out much worse…it could have turned out to be terminal. Sam Giancana's friends were not known to either be forgiving or to leave loose ends. Fortunately the mob hadn't found everything Will had hidden. They were satisfied they had everything when Will confessed to having a safety deposit box.

What he had managed to keep from revealing was the existence of an account in the Cayman Islands. The money would be enough for him to take the time to decide what to do next.

He did need to stay under the radar, however, and for nearly two years he did nothing. He rented an apartment on the beach at Grand Cayman and filled his days with rum and his nights with nubile young girls. But, like his adversary, Charlie Barron, he, too, wasn't cut out for permanent sloth. And with so much time elapsed, he felt it would be safe for him to go back. He moved a gym into his apartment, hired a trainer, and sweated himself into shape. It was time to enter the fray once again.

"Mr. Thompson, I hate to disturb you at lunch but you need to meet me."

Will Duval had moved out of his island apartment and returned to New York. He was staying at the Waldorf but the rates would begin to pinch if he didn't line something up soon. He had gone through a very significant amount of his stash. Harvey Thompson and Broadway Limited were his key.

"Then don't," Harvey said, wondering who this brash asshole disturbing his peace and quiet was?

"My name is Will Duval. I started California Cooking and I hate Charlie Barron as much as you do."

Harvey Thompson put his fork down and wiped his lips, staring at the dark, well-tanned man staring down at him.

"I'll see you in my office in one hour. Now get the fuck out of here and let me enjoy my meal."

"Pretty clever tracking me down. How did you do that?" Harvey asked as Will Duval sat down in the plush Broadway Limited office.

"I'm surprised you haven't seen me. I've been in and out of your Men's room, starting casual conversations or eavesdropping, trying to figure out how to meet you."

"Why not try the direct approach...make an appointment?"

"Would you have seen me?"

"Probably not," Harvey laughed. "You've got balls, that's for sure. Now, what is it you want?"

"I want to run the new operation you have in Los Angeles."

"You mean the one you scammed for the mob. News travels fast in our business."

"A different time...a different Will Duval."

"People don't change."

"I did...had to. Had the shit scared out of me. What didn't change was my certainty that I'm better than Charlie Barron at running a garment company and that's what you need."

"I don't like the man, and what he did to me, but it was enough years ago for me to let go...apparently you haven't."

"I can run a sportswear company...and I can run it cleanly and profitably. I can also put my feelings for Barron on the back burner. I'll find a way to take him down eventually but meanwhile I want to get back doing what I do best.

"You bought California Cooking...why I don't know, when you were already struggling with Starlet. Putting them together can reduce the bleeding but you still need to hype design, get people talking and build sales. Nothing fixes a problem like an increase in sales."

"With all due respect, you talk a good game but you've been out of it a couple of years and things have changed. Today it's more imports and fewer buyers."

"With all due respect," Will responded sarcastically. "Those are surface changes. It's still all about persuading buyers that you've got a better, prettier, and more efficient mousetrap. It's still about one-on-one selling. From what I've read about your background, you used to know that."

"Give me a few days," Harvey said, standing. "And stay the hell out of my men's room," he laughed as they both smiled.

Duval walked the four blocks to the 1407 and 1411 buildings he'd known so well. He took the elevator to the Galaxy showroom and entered.

"Hi, my name is Will Duval. I'm an old friend of Charlie Barron. Mind if I come in and look at your line?"

"Welcome, Mr. Duval. I am Adrienne. Would you like a drink?"

He watched her swivel away and it reminded him of the undulating waves of the Caribbean he's been watching the past two years.

"Adrienne will be busy for a short time while she's showing the line to a buyer," a young sales associate said, breaking Will's stare. "Is there something I can bring you?" she asked in a tone filled with nuances and inflections that made it difficult to keep from laughing. This girl was really young.

"Thanks, sweetheart. Please explain to Adrienne that I will be happy to wait until she's free."

Charlie sat for nearly an hour as he watched this dark-haired Italian beauty work her magic. The woman had that special something that intrigued women without making them jealous as she flirted extravagantly. But it was always with a point...the styles...the colors...getting an order far larger than that buyer had planned on writing.

"You are most patient," Adrienne said as the last buyers exited. They were the only two left in the showroom and the sudden silence added an unexpected sense to the moment as they looked at one another.

"I wouldn't have rushed Picasso," Will smiled. "He would have marveled at your prowess, the subtleties with which you weave your spell. You are mesmerizing. May I take you to dinner?"

It was a delightful late spring evening in Manhattan. Will took her hand. Adrienne only hesitated an instant before smiling at him. They held hands as if they'd been friends a long time as they walked downtown toward Chelsea and a small restaurant called Tinfoil. Couples overflowed onto the sidewalk and it took a $100 bill to get them a table.

"So how do you and Charlie know one another?" Adrienne said, sipping a Kir Royal, her eyes shining in the restaurant's subdued light, her hair dancing on her shoulders.

"We started in the business together. Ariana Fashions...crap garments...crap owner, but I learned a lot. It was a long time ago."

"And you and Charlie have remained friends all these years. That's really nice."

"Actually we hate each other's guts," he admitted, hoisting his glass in a mock toast. This was it. She'd either stay or walk out on him.

"I know!" She said smiling a very lascivious smile. "I know who you are. You are Mr. Will Duval of California Cooking and other mob-related businesses. I've always wanted to meet you."

"Why?" he asked, taken aback by her frankness.

"I couldn't believe all of Charlie's stories. No one could be that much of a shmuck."

"I've never heard anyone say 'shmuck' with an Italian accent. It's quite musical," he laughed. "At least you haven't walked out."

"Should I?"

"Of course not. We haven't eaten yet and it took me a C-note just to get our table. Let's continue. You can always leave."

Adrienne didn't leave. There was a risk in staying, but Will's charm and reputation excited her and when he invited her for a nightcap at his hotel, the Waldorf, she couldn't refuse. Charlie had told her about his various encounters with Will as he was busy seducing her shortly after he'd hired her to run the New York showroom.

They'd enjoyed one another occasionally when Charlie came to New York. He was a good lover. Not great...she'd definitely had better, but he paid her well, she liked her job, and if he thought it was one of his perks, she didn't mind. It never got serious.

But if Will was trouble, Charlie was certainly no saint...these are just two cocks in a ring brandishing their testosterone and measuring the size of their peckers. She'd known a lot of men like that. Sometimes it compensated for an embarrassingly small penis but Adrienne was pretty sure that Will, like Charlie, didn't suffer from that sort of an affliction.

A few hours later she was able to confirm that Will definitely had not been short changed. They'd gone from Tinfoil to the Waldorf penthouse for drinks and then to Will's room.

"My God, you're even better looking without clothes," Will marveled as he wiped his brow from the gymnastics of their lovemaking. "You should consider casting those breasts in bronze as a national treasure."

Adrienne laughed as she hopped out of bed. "I'm going to take a shower. I'm not sure this dampness is yours or mine."

"Probably comingled. I think I'll join you."

They squeezed into the Waldorf shower, smiling as he lifted her head and kissed her, the water spray splashing down on both their faces. Will felt himself getting hard again and Adrienne slid to her knees and took his penis in her mouth as Will fell against the back wall, his eyes closed, his senses transported as the water beat down on them.

Before he came, she stopped and led him into her. They both climaxed as the hot water disappeared and they giggled like children as the cold water chilled their ardor.

They grabbed warm towels and dried one another, snuggling under the covers and drifting off to sleep. The sound of the telephone's wake-up call at seven in the morning stirred them and a knock on the door a few minutes later with a call of "room service" moved them to action.

"What do you want, Will?" Adrienne asked as she buttered a croissant and sipped her coffee.

"Why would I want anything...except you, of course?"

"Because as much as I like you, you're trouble.   What are you doing these days?"

"I'm back heading a sportswear company.   Broadway Limited, who owns Starlet, has now bought California Cooking and I'm running the show."

"Congratulations, I guess.   They've taken two half-ass companies hoping to do what?"

"Cut costs, build sales...what we all try and do."

"And you wanted to see what Galaxy is doing," she said.

"But then I saw you and I didn't give a crap what Galaxy was doing.   Sounds like a bullshit line, but it's the truth. I'll be traveling between L.A. and New York.   I'd like to know that you and I are more than one night."

They never finished breakfast.   He spilled his coffee as he grabbed her and they kissed.   He untied both their robes and they stood together, naked, in front of the ceiling to floor window that looked out on to the city.

FOURTEEN

Windy

Within two years Galaxy had gained enough acceptances by major retailers to know it would survive. Charlie had called Paul Devine at Target. Paul invited him to Minneapolis and the two men went off for the weekend fishing and camping near a mountain lake. By the time Charlie flew back home, Paul had gotten him a coveted Vendor's number and given him a nice order. That order would mean a lot to the bottom line. This business will always be about relationships, Charlie mused, sitting back, sipping a Dewar's.

By the end of the third year Galaxy was successful enough for Charlie to have his own showroom in New York, twice as large as his first, and decorated with the finest Italian leather couches. It also hosted an extravagant buffet filled with fresh fruit, drinks, and snacks that were the envy of the entire building. Adrienne was quite at home in the larger showroom. She was now supervising two younger sales associates. Technically she was Adrienne Vincenzo but to her friends, she was Adrienne...and everyone was her friend.

Everyone included all women buyers and merchandisers

and all men over eighteen. There was even a small sign near the buffet that read "If you don't see it...ask for it (unless it's a condom...those you need to provide yourself)" It was followed by a happy face.

If you wanted to see a hot line and hot people, the Galaxy showroom was the place to be. In the afternoons you could just relax and kick back or have a drink. You could also go into a secluded alcove and snort a few lines. And, with all.the people around, you could often arrange for company that evening. The other showrooms thought about complaining to the building's management but they knew that there would be a backlash...the buyers who enjoyed Galaxy's largesse would hate them. One of the companies tried and lost half their business the following season. No one knew if that story was really true but the rumor was enough to squelch complaints.

Charlie was still unaware of the ongoing relationship between his New York showroom manager and Will Duval.

Unattached Charlie Barron moved casually from short relationship to short relationship. He went skiing with Brita, deep sea fishing with Candy, and to Vegas with Samantha. Then he met 'Windy' Green...unassuming 'Windy' Green...someone you would never imagine attracting Charles Barron...Ruth 'Windy' Green.

Ruth was 5'5" and average weight. She had a trim figure with breasts that were a little more than ample, but she was not what you'd consider knock-out attractive. Her friends called her 'Windy,' a carryover from her high school and college days surfing the Pacific Ocean beaches from Huntington north to Point Dune every chance she had.

Her most attractive feature was her amazing auburn hair and green eyes that made men look more than once.

At work she wore her hair in a conservative bun but when she unleashed it, her hair framed her face in a way that caused men to stare.

Ruth sold computers and had made an unsolicited sales call at Galaxy to see if they might be interested in a new system. Charlie had never been interested in such things but Ruth made it all sound so glamorous. He couldn't resist listening to her explain things in words that sung when she spoke them.

She was a Southern California girl, educated at UCLA. She still surfed when the weather was right and one month into meeting Charlie, she convinced him to try it. By then Charlie was calling her Windy as well.

Encouraged by his new girlfriend, Charlie moved to a place on the beach for the summer, just north of the lavish Malibu colony, home to an array of Hollywood's A-listers. Windy joined him, abandoning the apartment in Culver City she'd been sharing with, Willie, her older sister.

Willie had had a brief career as a model but now ran her own small modeling and talent agency that serviced a small coterie of local clients. It paid the rent. She was a slightly older version of Windy, darker hair, and a few inches taller but where Windy exuded pure energy, Willie exuded calm.

Willie wasn't thrilled that her younger sibling was dating an older man and even more upset that Windy had decided to move in with him, no matter how wealthy or enchanting this mystery Adonis was that Windy couldn't stop talking about.

Over the long Labor Day weekend, Charlie invited his children, Roger and Katie, to join him and Windy and to bring a friend if they desired. Katie brought a college girlfriend but Roger, a freshman at UC Santa Barbara, brought a girlfriend, Sarah. Willie also came, but solo. Sleeping arrangements were turning out to be complicated. Roger wanted to bed down with Sarah, demanding adult status.

"For Christ's sake, Roger," Charlie pleaded. "I can't have you sleep with Sarah under my roof. Your mother would go ballistic."

"Then don't tell her. And while we're at it, your new girlfriend is only a few years older than I am. Aren't you doing a little crib-robbing here?"

"Forget Windy. She and I are both adults."

"Maybe you…I'm not sure about her," Roger teased.

"You take the couch and we'll let the four women figure out their own arrangements. Please," he begged.

The next morning Windy led them all down to the water's edge and began showing them how to surf. Willie and Charlie stood off to one side.

"Aren't you going in?" Charlie asked. "You look great in that swimsuit."

Willie looked at him. Charlie had an animal appeal that was hard to resist and if he wasn't involved with her kid sister, she'd give in.   This was a man who sent signals indiscriminately and she was picking them up. Christ, he's attractive.

"No, I think I'll go in and fix breakfast for everyone," she said, deciding it was safer to not stand in such close proximity to her host.

Charlie stood there, looking out at Windy riding her board, bent over in what he guessed was a perfect position, a huge wave behind her, framing her auburn hair in the morning sun. The others were cheering her on.

"I'll join you," he said, unsure whether that was the right decision, knowing the erection pushing his trunks could lead him into a delicate situation.

He was nursing a Bloody Mary as he watched Willie take a tray of eggs from the refrigerator and begin cracking them. He could see that her hands were shaking slightly.

"Here, take a sip of this," he said, coming up alongside of her.

"Char..." were all the words she got out before she was in his embrace and they were kissing. It felt so right and she let herself go. The kiss lingered, the Bloody Mary and the eggs forgotten. When they finally separated, she just looked into his eyes. They were smiling.

"This is so wrong," Willie said. "I'm going to leave before my sister and your children come back."

"Please don't leave. We can explain our feelings to them," he argued.

"Windy adores you and I adore my sister. This could destroy everything she and I have together and I won't do that. You do what you have to but promise me you won't hurt her. I'd never forgive you if you did and then we'd never have a chance."

She turned and ran from the room. Ten minutes later he heard a car drive away.

"Where's Willie?" Windy asked as the small group returned to the house, laughing, hair askew, bodies full of sand.

"She got a telephone call and then said she had to leave. I'm starving. I started to crack some eggs. You guys up for breakfast?"

"Dad, you shouldn't have left us. Windy is an amazing surfer. She even taught clumsy me," Roger said. He'd become so taken with his father's girlfriend that Sarah, the girl he'd brought, stood alone off to one side, pouting.

"C'mon, Sarah...help me make breakfast. Was the water too cold?" Charlie asked, hoping to bring her into the conversation. He was still struggling to figure out what had happened between him and Willie and what he was now supposed to do about Windy. I'm getting too old for this complicated high school sort of shit, he said to himself.

By Monday evening things were calmer. Roger had returned his attentions to Sarah once he saw his father pay attention to her. Windy knew something was amiss. She and Charlie were still having sex and she had even introduced some new things but that special excitement that comes from the first few times you're with someone was gone. Maybe that was all there was, Windy reasoned. Nothing she tried seemed to work. And why had Willie left?

The middle of the following week, Charlie met Ruby for dinner. They got together at least once a month on the excuse of talking about the kids and finances. They still loved one another and maybe this was better than being married.

"Roger tells me you have a new girlfriend...a hot surfer chick," Ruby teased.

"Don't listen to him...he's a teenage boy with raging hormones," Charlie said, sipping a special Cabernet that he knew Ruby liked. "Besides, the girl he was referring to, Ruth Green, and I were only dating and that's over."

"Do I say I'm sorry, or was she just another notch on your gun belt?"

"I'm not that bad, am I Ruby?"

"Charlie, if you were much younger, I'd just say you were incorrigible. Now I just think of you as Peter Pan, the boy who never wanted to grow up."

"You know that maturity is highly overrated."

"The way you lead your life, it certainly is."

"Anyone new in your life?" he asked, eager to change the subject.

"No one I'd care to discuss but I've decided to spend a month in Nassau with a girlfriend. I want to get away and I hope you'll be able to spend more time with Katie and Roger. My aunt will be at the house while I'm gone but it will ease my mind if I know the kids can count on you if something comes up."

"Of course. Maybe I'll join you for a few days. I have to go to Miami at some point on business and visit Jordan Marsh."

"I'd rather you didn't," she said without explanation.

"Willie, Charlie Barron! Good morning," he said, calling her office.

"Good morning, Charlie," she said, nervously.

"Will you have dinner with me tonight?"

"Not a good idea. You and Windy are still involved." "Not so. We broke it off Saturday. She needs someone younger and I need someone older."

"Charlie...please! Give it a month. If we see one another now she'll believe I was the cause. Will you call me again?"

"Absolutely. Count on it," he said, upset. He had never been good with rejection.

He never called again.

It took several meetings in New York and Los Angeles before Charlie was able to get a meeting with Walmart.

The behemoth company was headquartered in Bentonville, Arkansas...not exactly the fashion capitol of the country. The Walton family had applied considerable political pressure to have the Federal government build a modern airport in this old bastion of the Confederacy. The only passengers arriving were there to visit Walmart or buy frozen chickens.

One would have thought that black faces would be dominant in this small southern community but they were actually the exception. The large local Super Walmart store had few African American employees and fewer customers. Charlie's meeting the next day was held in a small, sterile Quonset hut recycled from the Second World War that had ended nearly three decades earlier.

"Can I take you to lunch?" Charlie asked the three buyers sitting across from him.

"Thank you, but we're not permitted. Please, show us your line. We've heard a lot of good things about your company."

As Charlie nervously pulled various groups from his bag, they asked a lot of questions.

"Where do you manufacture these? What is the exact fabric content? We know your sell price but if you change this sleeve and that pocket, you could reduce your price and then we might be interested. How many wash cycles before colors fade?" And, on and on.

Two hours later, they thanked him...asked him to leave six styles and walked out.

"We'll let you know in two weeks, Mr. Barron."

Flummoxed...Charlie thought of a word he rarely used. He was depleted. Selling these white bread buyers in their backyard was a daunting task.

The Walmart buyers never called nor responded to Charlie's telephone calls. They also never returned the six styles they were interested in, but six weeks later Bunny found the same styles hanging in their store. They were hard to miss. Walmart hadn't even bothered to change the color palette.

"I'd love to sue those bastards," Charlie said when Bunny walked wordlessly into his office and set the six garments down, side by side. She'd purchased them at the Walmart in the San Fernando Valley.

"K-Mart did the same thing to a girl friend of mine who works for Tremulo. They asked to see the line...asked them to leave a few pieces, and then knocked them off."

Galaxy now had individual designers for its line of Junior tops, Knits, and Dresses. Bunny oversaw them all, leaving behind half-empty red Coca-Cola cans in her wake as she moved constantly between shopping the stores for the latest trends and commenting on what the designers were putting together.

"I'm going to open my own retail store...high end, on Montana," Charlie announced to Bunny, David Ryan, Sales Manager for his dress division, Lindsay Stuart, Manager of his Knit Division, and his old friend, Bruce Goslin, who was now overseeing his Junior Division. Charlie had finally convinced Bruce to move to Los Angeles and, after a bad marriage that had struggled through five years, two children and an emptied checking account, he gave in.

"You don't have enough aggravation," Bunny said. "You are crazy...certifiable! You've got Galaxy doing well..."

"Not well enough," Charlie interrupted. "I want you to create a new label...Charlie, and find a designer who can do couturier."

"Charlie has been taken...Revlon used it for perfume...remember?" Bruce laughed. "How about Baroness? If you need to stroke your ego that might do it."

"I like it...Baroness...but spell it with two n-s...I don't want it to be confused."

"Charlie...misspelling the word is really an ego trip...settle for one 'n'," David Ryan said, sharing in the fun.

"OK, fuck you all...one 'n' but I found this terrific space near Euclid, north side of the street, two thousand square feet. I want to open by early November. Can we do that, Bunny?"

"Why not? I have nothing else going on," she said sarcastically. "I'll get a new designer; you get the store set up."

"OK, that's settled. I was looking at the figures this morning. What happened, David? You've had massive returns from Plymouth, Brooks, and a couple of others."

Lindsay, Bruce, and Bunny started laughing so hard that tears were rolling down their cheeks. David looked like a young boy caught in the act of fondling himself and the more his associates laughed, the redder his face became.

"What the hell is going on?" Charlie asked. "Is someone going to let me in on this joke that isn't funny? We've got a return of several hundred garments."

"Can I explain it?" Lindsay asked. "Please. I doubt that David can do it justice."

"I don't give a fuck who tells me...someone...anyone."

"Alright," she said, smothering her laughter. "You're always picking on David to bring in more business...sell more accounts. So..." she started laughing again. "I'm sorry. OK! He decided to go all out. 'I'll show Charlie how to bring in orders' he bragged.

"He spent a lot of extra time on each of these four accounts because they could write major orders. He got romantic with each of the buyers...even told them he loved them and as you know as well as anyone...great sex often leads to great orders."

"He fucked all four buyers?" Charlie asked, not sure whether to join the laughter or scream in anger.

"Yup," Lindsay continued.

"I didn't know that these women were all friends. For Christ's sakes, Charlie. It was an innocent mistake," David whined.

"David…I love you but you fucked up big this time and it's an expensive mistake," Charlie frowned.

"How could I know they would brag to one another about an innocent affair?

"Don't give yourself too much credit," Lindsay added. "The way I understand it, it was more than a couple of nights. You implied a lot more, and you know we women always like to compare notes on how dumb men can be. They figured out the same, good looking, tousle-haired stud had done them all. That's when they decided to get even. Voila …big orders…late cancellations."

"David," Charlie said, exasperated, not knowing whether to laugh or cry.

"Charlie," David spoke up, an apologetic tone in his voice, trying to defend himself. "You've never screwed a buyer?"

"Of course, I have, but not four women at the same time who also happen to be girlfriends. I ought to take the cost of these garments out of your commission but you are so overdrawn already we'd be into the next century before you break even. Now get out of here…all of you. And, Bunny…hire a good designer."

David Ryan was young and adorable, with curly light brown hair…the kind of hair women love to run their fingers through. He was a drop-out from a local Junior

College. In high school he'd been a Second string basketball player, a second string baseball player, and a second-rate student. But his father, a mediocre seller of notions...those buttons and zippers that were so necessary to complete a garment, got him a job shuffling paper at a local manufacturer.

When Charlie met David, two years later, he knew instantly that the kid had that special magic. David had been under his wing ever since. David could make lots of mistakes...and did, but to Charlie they were all mistakes he'd made when he was younger...mistakes that could be forgiven. Shagging four buyers on the same trip was just such a forgivable goof.

At the other end of Galaxy's management team was Lindsay Stuart, his Knit Division manager. She was an experienced pro. She had trained as a buyer at Neiman, Marcus. Then she came over to the dark side, selling for Calvin Klein. Lindsay was good. She knew people and knew that what her buyers needed was accurate information and not bull shit. They wanted to be kept abreast of two things. 'Would we be shipping on time or be late and what was 'checking?' Success was often achieved by being able to reorder a style that was selling well, maybe even bring it in the following season in a different fabric or color.

Lindsay was also thorough and very private in her public persona. If she slept around...and everyone wondered, she was discrete. Even Charlie didn't know...and he tried. Lindsay was 5'8"...nearly 6' in heels, and she loved to wear heels. Men didn't intimidate her but with her tawny skin and high cheek bones, she knew she was a lot of men's fantasy...a tall, light-skinned, mixed race, beauty. If you were going to get involved with Lindsay, you'd better be serious. To her Charlie and David were boys, not men. Charlie was a little older, a little more suave, but they were both going to remain boys that would never grow up. Neither of them were Lindsay's type.

Lindsay's mother, Phyllis, had escaped from Mississippi after her father was lynched. He'd been accused of staring at a white woman. There was no trial. The woman complained to her husband, a crowd gathered, and within an hour it was all over. Mrs. Stuart grabbed Lindsay and her younger brother and caught the first train to Chicago where she could eke out a living in safer surroundings. Phyllis made all of her daughter's clothes but early on Lindsay insisted on adding design touches. The girl definitely had an eye and it got her a scholarship to New York's Fashion Institute.

Bunny ran ads for a new Designer and reached out to all her connections but the women and men who applied, gay and straight, Persian, Oriental, Latino or white didn't seem to have what she was looking for. She wasn't sure she had that special panache either but like every designer she'd ever known, she yearned to work on something 'better ...something a little different.'

"I can do that job," she told Papa. They were standing on the shipping platform where Bunny could smoke without getting hollered at, a fresh can of Coke in her other hand. "I'm going to promote from within. You know Lorena Gonzalez, that young, pretty, Latina girl who's been an Assistant doing blouses. She's ready. I'm going to promote her to run the Junior Division and I'll do the line for the new store until I find just the right person."

Papa just nodded. It was a part of the business totally foreign to him but he knew Bunny liked to think out loud and he was her favorite listening post.

Lorena Gonzalez was elated and she knew her father, Rodrigo, who managed Galaxy's fabric inventory would be very proud. He'd even gotten her the job, her first job after graduating from the local Fashion Institute.

Audrey Milton, Charlie's old bookkeeper, was now functioning as Controller of Galaxy...trying to keep Charlie's tumultuous business life in some sort of order.

With David and Lindsay close behind her, they approached Charlie a few days later on another matter.

"Since you've decided to expand again without any proper planning, you need to get Lili some help managing production," Audrey said.

"So, get someone, I need to get out of here. I'm leaving for a few days. Someone new. I'll be in Vegas at Caesar's. Don't call me."

"Who is she?" David asked.

"Her name is Tanya. She's a dancer in the Hallelujah Hollywood show at the MGM. I met her last fall at the MAGIC show when I was there."

The three of them smiled.

"Tell me more, oh Master of the Horizontal Kingdom," David laughed.

"I will say no more so as to not tarnish the lady's reputation."

"She has a reputation?" Lindsay added, her eyes twinkling. "Is that something new for you, Charlie?"

"Charlie, we all want to know if you'd consider hiring Sid Strauss?"

"Sid Strauss? Sid Strauss of the Manny, Mo, & Jack fuck-up group?" Charlie laughed, falling back into his chair. "Are you kidding? Sid, Larry, and Tom had a terrific company going, Harbor Apparel. In one weekend they managed to destroy everything they'd been building for two years and now all three have had to file for bankruptcy."

"I didn't realize all that," Lindsay said. "What happened?"

"The three of them were equal partners. Sid had even married Larry's sister and they'd recently had twins. Anyway, Larry ran sales, Sid ran production, and Tom sort of oversaw the operation. Last year...on a Friday, Larry sets up a meeting with his two partners and tells them that he's really the key to Harbor's success and should own more than a third of the business. They tell him that they'll think about it over the weekend and let him know on Monday.

"Monday comes and the two guys announce to Larry that they'd given his proposal considerable thought and, instead of increasing his ownership percentage, they'd decided to fire him."

"Can they do that?" Audrey asked as they had all taken seats, rapt by the lunatic story.

"They owned two-thirds of the business, so they could...and they did," Charlie continued. "But now comes the best part. All three had guaranteed the finances of the business to Heller Financial, the factor that owned all their accounts receivable. Larry would be gone but he would still be liable. Within six months the other two ran the business into the ground and all three men had to file for bankruptcy."

"Wow," Lindsay said, taking a breath. "Amazing!"

"There's more," Charlie smiled, warming to the telling of the story. "Your friend Sid, was having an affair with a girl. I think her name was Tippy. He gets her pregnant and bails on his wife and two infants...remember, the wife was Larry's sister, so now Larry is ready to put out a contract on the shmuck.

"Tom discovers he has cancer and disappears into a medical abyss, and Larry, not to be outdone, is discovered to be having an affair with a buyer in New York when his wife begins listening in to their phone calls.

"Sid and Tippy end up with twins so now he's supposed to be paying child support for four children under the age of four. They run away to the East Coast and he decides to bury himself by becoming an Orthodox Jew, studying and not working."

"Charlie, is this all your fabled bullshit?" Lindsay asked, roaring with laughter.

"Even I couldn't make this stuff up. This should be a television story on America's Biggest Fuck-ups. Tell them, David...is this true?"

"I didn't know the full story, but Tippy told me a similar story before she became the mother of twins and ran away with Sid three thousand miles from his earlier responsibilities."

"So I guess that means you don't want to consider hiring Sid," Audrey said, maintaining her dour voice.

"That's what I've always liked about you, Audrey...you are such a quick study. Now I'm out of here. Enjoy your weekend. I will."

FIFTEEN

Baroness

The opening of Baroness in Santa Monica was a hit as hundreds of Charlie's friends and curious shoppers crowded the store, sipping champagne and nibbling canapés from Thursday evening's grand opening through a blazing sunset on Sunday. A small piano set up on the sidewalk entertained in a manner never seen on the upscale street.

The Los Angeles Times sent a reporter and photographer to capture the event and a full-page spread publicized the store. It was picked up by the New York papers and became an industry sensation. Charlie Barron was becoming a brand.

"Mr. Barron?" A month after the successful opening of Baroness, Charlie still basking in the glow, a well-dressed man stopped by the offices of Galaxy and asked to see him. The man was ushered in and Charlie got out from behind his desk to greet him.

"You wanted to see me?"

"Yes. You are Charlie Barron?"

"Of course," he said curtly. "What can I do for you?"

"You've been served," the man smiled, handing Charlie an envelope. Quickly he turned and left without another word.   "You ass-hole...come back here."

Charlie turned and sat down, tearing open the envelope.

He stared for a moment and then let out a huge animal scream.

"Get me Tom Snyder on the phone," he shouted.

"They say he's in a meeting" came a disembodied voice from a desk outside his office.

"Tell them to get him the fuck out of his meeting...**NOW**!"

Minutes passed and Charlie's anger increased.

"He's on!"

"Tom, I'm being charged with criminal rape. This is bullshit. Calm down? How the fuck can I calm down? Can you come here? Never mind...I'm coming to your office," he said, slamming down the receiver, not waiting for a reply.

Charlie stormed into the law offices of O'Reilly, Snyder and Lipschitz, a something for everyone law firm in the Union Bank building. Charlie had been approached by several larger firms through the years...more prestigious ones, but Tom Snyder had always been there for him and Charlie appreciated loyalty.

"This cocksucking Vegas lawyer says he represents a girl named Melanie Sutton, a girl I knew as Tanya. He claims the girl was underage when I forced her to have sex and now she's pregnant."

"And?" Tom asked, hoping his client would eventually take a breath and calm down.

"And, what? I met the girl at MAGIC last fall. She was modeling. She said she was nineteen and worked as a dancer at the MGM in the Hollywood show. A few months ago we spent a weekend together. That's all I know."

"Did you use a condom?"

"Of course," Charlie insisted.

"Every time?"

"I can't be sure," he admitted. "But it sure as shit wasn't rape...she was more than a willing participant."

"Not if she was under eighteen," Tom reminded his friend. "If she was under eighteen, you might be in deep trouble."

"The girl had size forty tits...no way was she a child."

"And you checked her ID?"

"Of course not. It never even dawned on me. Tom, I do a lot of fucked up things in my life but messing with someone close to the age of my daughter has never been my style. I'm telling you Tanya, or Melanie, or whatever her name is, knew her way around a bedroom."

"Let me contact her lawyer. They haven't contacted the Vegas police.   It sounds like they are in this purely for money. If she was a minor...it will cost you, but I doubt it ever becomes a criminal event."

"David, I need you to do me a favor...a personal one."

"Sure, Charlie. But before you tell me, I want to show you this picture of the new Porsche Targa I ordered ...special sports package, new alloy wheels and a stereo package that will blow your mind."

"David, you need a $70,000 car like you need another hole in your head. Does your wife know?"

"Sure, Carol knows. I told her. She smiled, and walked away shaking her head but, hell, she'll be fine."

"I'm on her side.   Do you ever save money for tomorrow?" Charlie asked.

"I will...tomorrow! " David laughed.   "Now, what's the errand you need?"

"I want you to go to Vegas and connect up with this girl. Her name is Tanya and she works at the MGM but her real name may be Melanie Sutton. She says I raped her. She also says she was jail bait when it happened. I need you to find out what it will take to make her go away. My lawyer is talking to her lawyer but this might be quicker and cheaper."

"Can I leave after I get my Porsche on Friday?"

"No, damn it. I need this done ASAP and, David...one more thing. She's also claiming she's pregnant."

David made the three hundred mile drive in just over four hours using his radar detector to avoid the California Highway Patrol cars hiding near Barstow. Charlie had given him Tanya's telephone number. It was an answering service but David was able to make arrangements to meet her after the MGM show ended just before midnight. Her pregnancy wasn't keeping her from working both jobs.

"David?" she said as she slithered into the booth at the MGM lounge bar. "Don't stand up. Were you able to catch the show?" Tanya was nearly six feet tall in flats and had the body of a showgirl with large breasts and hips that moved sensuously. She had ash blonde hair, long, resting casually on her shoulders. Experience told David it wasn't her natural color. She struck him more as 'mousy brown.'

"No, sorry I had to miss it. I did catch it last year though...thirty gorgeous girls and sixty of the prettiest boobs I've seen in a long time." He smiled his David smile and she returned it comfortably.

"Do you have a room, David? We can go up now if you like."

"I do. But let's chat for a few minutes."

"OK. What would you like to 'chat' about?" she said, putting a special nuance on the word 'chat.'

"Charlie Barron," he said softly, resting his arm on hers as he could feel her freeze up and start to leave. "Don't leave…please. I'm here as a friend."

"Talk to my lawyer. I don't want to talk about this. You misled me." There were tears in the corner of her eyes.

"Look, Charlie sent me here. He's not a bad guy. I think you know that. He wants to be fair. If this thing ever goes to trial, both your reputations will be ruined. I understand your name is Melanie…can I call you Melanie? Where are you from?"

David could feel her begin to relax.

"Indiana. A small town near Terre Haute! My father works at the Columbia Records factory there. My mother teaches the 2d Grade. Charlie was a nice guy but my lawyer…an ex-boyfriend, found out he was rich and convinced me we could tap him. It wasn't something I wanted."

"What do you want, Melanie? I mean, really want."

"I always wanted to be an actress, maybe in the movies, maybe the stage, but I couldn't afford acting classes. We don't make much money being showgirls but the side benefits are good." They both understood what the side benefits were. Charlie had paid her $500 for the weekend, more than two weeks' salary strutting around a stage, bare-chested in 3" heels six nights a week.

"Charlie said he'd give you $50,000.00 to drop this matter and leave Las Vegas. You can come to Los Angeles or go to New York. Either place, he knows some people and will get you introductions. Interested?"

David watched her eyes light up and her mind racing through all the things such an offer could mean.

"He'd really do that? This isn't a gag...I drop the lawsuit and then he changes his mind?" she asked, her breath coming faster.

"No, nothing like that. I have a paper you can sign and I'll give you a check. You can drive to L.A. with me or I'll take you to the airport and put you on a plane for New York. I can also arrange for a place for you to stay once you get there."

Seconds passed and it was if they were alone and the hundreds of gamblers and drinkers around them had disappeared. David sat quite still. He was a skilled salesman and he knew enough to stop talking and wait.

"New York!" she said softly. "I want to go to New York."

"Then New York it will be. There is a direct flight leaving tomorrow at noon, will that work?"

"This is real? This is really happening?"

"Yes," he said. Charlie had told him he could offer her as much as $100,000.00, if necessary. "Now, would you like to have a late supper?"

"Let's go to your room. As long as I'm giving up this life, we might as well both enjoy the evening. This one will be on me," she laughed.

"The baby probably wasn't yours," David smiled as he sat across from Charlie, the signed letter handed over.

"Was she underage?"

"That I can't swear to but she was a great piece of ass," David laughed.

"Yes, she was...yes, she was."

Starlet Fashions was beginning to make inroads into Galaxy's success. Will had hired good sales people and a young designer from Barcelona. She designed garments that worked for her and her age group. Will set her up to email what she was doing and ended up with thousands of followers and trendsetters...high school and college girls who doted on looking outrageously new. By their standards Galaxy was old school.

Every few weeks Will traveled to New York. He claimed it was for business but as often as not it was to see Adrienne. He'd arrange to arrive on Wednesday, do a little business and then hustle her off to the Hamptons for a long weekend. They'd worked hard to keep their arrangement private. Charlie wouldn't be pleased. But nothing is forever.

It was time for Roger Barron to get some work experience. He was between his Junior and Senior years at the University of California at Santa Barbara and had grown to be an inch taller than his father with dark, wavy hair, a pronounced Adam's apple, and a cleft in his chin. He was willowy...one would worry about him in a strong wind. But he had his father's smile and his abundance of self-confidence.

"Come to work at the factory," Charlie told him.

"Dad, I don't want to be in L.A. for the summer. Let me go back to New York. I've only been there once and that was when I was twelve. I can work in the showroom."

"Your mother will skin me alive letting you loose on an innocent Manhattan." He knew it was an argument a parent couldn't win. My son wants to spread his wings. I did when I was his age...that and a lot more, he mused. "I'll call Adrienne and let her know she has a new employee to train but," he emphasized, "Don't give her any grief."

"So, Adrienne, how about showing me some of the good spots in New York?" Roger asked, his first day in the showroom. He'd come in an hour late and whether he had any intention of working was open to question. Clearly he didn't think of himself as just another sales associate and the rest of the showroom staff was unsure how to treat the owner's son.

"Another time, Roger," she said. "We've got a busy week...lots of appointments and by the end of the day I'm usually exhausted."

"Sure. I understand. How about this weekend?"

"Let's see how the week goes. Now, we've got to straighten up. Lord and Taylor's buyer will be here soon.

Grab those garments and get them hung on the display, will you?"

"For you, dear Adrienne, anything."

She recognized the tone. He was becoming smitten with her and that meant trouble. Just what she needed...a pubescent kid just out of teens AND Charlie's son. She was already breaking out in a rash juggling her relationship with Will. Maybe that was why Galaxy had lost three sizeable orders to Starlet. Maybe she was losing her mojo...not focusing.

And now both David and Charlie were asking questions. She didn't have any good answers. She'd shopped the stores where Starlet was hanging. The garments looked good...not great, but solid. There had to be a reason. She worried that it had something to do with her relationship with Will but she made sure they never discussed the line or the customers. But, really, who would believe her when sales started declining?

She and Will were having dinner at Tinfoil a month later when they looked over at a corner booth and saw Roger with three girls and another guy. The girls looked like 'hookers.'

They were definitely not NYU students. When Adrienne told Will who it was, he froze, and a look came over his face that she had never seen before. It felt strange.

"Are we getting away this weekend?" she asked. No reply!

"Will, I asked if we were getting away this weekend," she said, snapping her fingers in front of his face.

"Excuse me, hon...I'll be right back...Men's room," he said, bolting from the table.

"Hey, buddy," Will said, standing at the sink next to Roger Barron. "You've got some white stuff on your upper lip. You may want to clean it up before you go back to your table."

The younger man stared in the mirror. "I'm not seeing it."

"Here," Will said. "In the corner. You know, I can supply you with some Grade-A blow at a great price if you're interested. My name is Chaz," he said sticking his hand out.

"Roger...Roger Barron. I don't know...I use occasionally but it's always been my friend's stash."

"Not right to always take from your friends, Roger. That's OK for chics but guys need to put up their own once in a while."

"Maybe another time. I need to get back."

"I understand...but before you do, try a line of this...free. It'll take you to the moon and beyond."

Roger hesitated for a minute and then bent down. He had cleared a line in one nostril when Adrienne swung open the door to the Men's Room.

"What's going on here? Roger stop...get the hell out of here or I'll let your father know what the fuck you're doing?"

"Adrienne?" Roger said, stunned, looking up, his eyes red. "What are you doing here? This is the Men's room...I think," he laughed. "Besides, I'm 20. Want some...Meet Chaz, he's a fun guy to know."

Adrienne stared at Will when a man tried to enter.

"Get the fuck out of here," she shouted. "Can't you see we're busy?

"Roger, I need you to leave...now. Please leave and take a cab to your apartment. Don't even stop at your table or I'll make sure your ass is on the first plane tomorrow heading west. You hear me?"

The tall no-longer teenager sulked from the bathroom and past the small crowd that was gathering to see what the ruckus was.

Will just stood there, blinking, wondering what he'd just done...wondering if it was worth it.

"Get the fuck out of my way," Adrienne said, pushing her way through the throng of mostly men anxiously waiting to empty their bladders. She reached her table and confirmed that Roger had done as she'd asked...left directly without returning to his table.

Then she heard screams and shouting from the front of the restaurant and something told her she had to get there. She pushed her way through the crowd...through the front door to flashing red lights and gawkers blocking the sidewalk.

"What happened? Let me through?"

"Some guy got hit by a cab going downtown while he was crossing the street to catch a cab going uptown...must have never looked where he was going."

"Let me through...please," Adrienne pleaded to the policeman trying to hold the crowd back. "I think that's my friend...please."

"What's your friend's name?"

"Roger...Roger Barron."

"Hey, Sarge! Lady says it might be her friend...Roger Barron. That him?"

The policeman in charge nodded and Adrienne was allowed through as a body was being lifted onto a gurney.

"Is he alive? Please, tell me he's alive," she said, tears flowing down her cheeks, blackened by mascara.

"Barely."

"Can I go to the hospital with him? He works for me and I'm a close friend of his father."

The ride to the hospital seemed to last forever. Adrienne held Roger's hand while the ER Medics tried to keep him alive. They weren't successful. Just as the ambulance reached the hospital the two white coated men nodded their heads sadly.

"I'm sorry Ma'am.   We tried.   That cab hit him full on...too much internal bleeding."

Adrienne fell across Roger's body, sobbing.

Charlie and Ruby arrived the next morning.   They'd taken the red-eye but had slept very little on the six hour flight.   They had also spoken very little to one another, their shared tragedy keeping their anger in check.

Adrienne met them at the airport and together they went to the morgue where their son's body was awaiting formal identification.

"I'm going to sue the fucking cabbie that hit him...son-of-a-bitch...my son, dead, crossing the street," Charlie ranted.

Adrienne remained silent, understanding there was a lot more to Roger's death than being struck by a cab.

"Your son had a great deal of cocaine in his system," the Doctor told them.   .   "The impact from the taxi killed him, but his senses had already been severely impaired."

"Are you saying he was high?" Charlie asked.

"In lay terms, Mr. Barron, your son was stoned. He may not have even known he was in the middle of the street."

"You let him come here, you son-of-a-bitch," Ruby screamed, collapsing into a chair, sobbing uncontrollably. "You thought he was old enough to be on his own. You killed our son...you killed our son."

Charlie tried to say something, to comfort her, but then understood there was nothing he could say. His son was dead and something inside him was dying as well.

It took a few days to arrange for Roger's body to be flown back to Los Angeles. Ruby remained in her hotel room, locked in seclusion, until she could accompany her son's casket on his last flight. Charlie moved into the company's apartment going to the showroom once or twice but showing no interest in what was going on.

People came up to him to extend their condolences but they were talking to a man who was there in body only. He planned to return to Los Angeles on the same plane as Ruby but she had demanded they not sit next to one another.

"Before you leave I need to tell you more about what happened that night," Adrienne said, taking Charlie aside just before he prepared to depart for the airport. There were a few people milling around the showroom.

"I don't know if I want to know any more details. My son got stoned and got himself killed. You happened to be there and tried to get him out. I'm grateful but it doesn't change anything."

"Sit your ass down, Charlie. I don't know if I'll have the courage to say what I'm going to say after today. I'm quitting. I'm going back to Italy. I'm sad...very sad, and I feel guilty as well. You are probably going to hate me by the time I finish and I won't blame you. I'm not too proud of myself at this point either."

Charlie sat down and waited while Adrienne instructed the sales people to leave and close up the showroom. She didn't want anyone to hear what she was going to say.

"I've been seeing Will Duval. No...no...don't get angry or say anything until I'm finished," she said, knowing she had already crossed the Rubicon.

"I've been very careful keeping my personal relationship separate from the business. We never talked about styles, or fabrics, or customers. But at this point you can believe that or not because it's over...everything is over," she said, her voice cracking as she wiped the tears from her cheek.

"Will and I were having dinner at Tinfoil, a restaurant in Chelsea, when I saw Roger and four of his friends at another table. They were drinking and doing coke in the open. I mentioned to Will who Roger was and the moment Roger got up to go to the Men's Room, Will bolted from the table and followed him.

"I waited, not knowing what to do, but when neither of them came back I went into the Men's Room, not really giving a shit about protocol. Will had given Roger some bullshit name and convinced him to shoot another line. I'm guessing that's what put Roger over the top.

"I began shouting to Roger to get the fuck out of there and go directly to his hotel. He left as I asked him to do, not even stopping at his table. When I heard hollering from the front of the restaurant I ran out. Roger was lying on the street."

Charlie sat, his face taut and icy as Adrienne slumped into a nearby chair, sobbing. Minutes passed. Charlie's hands shook as he clenched and unclenched his fists. His eyes were red when he stood.

"Get one of your associates back in here and give them your keys. Then take your things and go wherever in the fuck you want to go. You can go to hell if you can get a flight...anywhere but here. If we owe you anything we'll send it to you. Now, please get the fuck out of my sight before I forget you're a lady and I'm a gentleman."

Charlie never made his flight nor the next one or the one after that. He left a message for Ruby at her home asking her to make funeral arrangements. He'd be back for their son's burial.

"Harvey, this is Charlie Barron. Can we meet somewhere?"

"Charlie, I heard about your son. I'm very sorry. Can you tell me what we need to discuss?"

"It's personal. Please, indulge me. I know we aren't friends but it's quite important."

"Harry's Bar on 14th Street, 5 PM....I'll be there," Charlie confirmed, hanging up. He looked in the mirror and didn't recognize the red-eyed, unshaven face staring back at him. He smelled like hell. He threw off all his clothes and moved to the shower. He had the beginning of a plan.

Harvey Thompson sat back in his chair wondering what the hell this was all about. He thought about calling Will

Duval to see if he had any ideas but decided against it. Harvey's curiosity was piqued.

Harvey Thompson was nursing a vodka seven when Charlie walked in, adjusted his eyes to the dim light, and spotted Harvey waiting for him in a corner booth.

"Hello Harvey. It's been a long time since our meetings in Neil's office and my departure from Starlet. Thanks for meeting me."

"Curiosity. You fucked me over but it was a long time ago and it seems to finally be turning out. Your friend, Will Duval, is doing a good job."

"Black label, neat...make it a double," Charlie said to the waitress, smiling and hovering at the edge of the table.

"Will Duval killed my son and I want your help to make him pay for it. I want him out of my life, forever," Charlie emphasized.

"I'm sure you're going to tell me why I'm going to help you," Harvey said, trying to retain his calm. This isn't the brash Charlie Barron he'd met years ago. This is an angry, distraught father seeking revenge. "First, tell me why you think Will killed your son."

"He's been having an affair with the woman, Adrienne, who ran my New York showroom until I fired her two days ago. The two of them were having dinner when they spotted my son. Adrienne knew Roger...he'd been working at the showroom during the summer. She pointed him out to Will.

"Will followed my son into the Men's Room and Adrienne followed a few minutes later. Will had given the boy a false name and a lot of cocaine. The kid had already had a little. Will's put him over the top. I know Will hates me...always has, and I'm not too fond of him but transferring that hate to my son Is unacceptable."

"I agree. So, you kill him. Why should I help you?"

"I'll give you two reasons...pick your preference."

"First, I know about your Mafia connections...your silent partners. I also know about your offshore bank accounts. You do more than marlin fishing on your vacations. Second, your boy, Will, not only uses coke, he deals in it...a little side business of his. That business probably competes with some of your partners in a way that wouldn't make them happy.

"And, now as I think of it, I've got a third reason. I'm prepared to put everything I've got, or can borrow, into selling Broadway Limited stock short...at least two million dollars. Your partners might not like that either and start asking questions. Do I need any more?"

"Why haven't you used this alleged information before?"

"Why? I don't dislike you. I never did. I've always admired how you built Broadway Limited. You did a terrific job. And I never cared what Will Duval did. On an even playing field I knew I could beat him. But he changed that...forever."

"And, assuming I believe everything you say..."

"You do, Harvey…you do!"

"As I was saying, if I believe everything you say, would you be satisfied if I just removed Mr. Duval from your life?"

"I would."

"And that's the end of the story…no more threats."

"I'd have no reason, Harvey."

"Thank you, Charlie. Have a good return flight to Los Angeles and please give my deepest sympathies to your wife."

"Good night, Harvey."

Charlie slept the entire flight to Los Angeles remembering a very early lesson…don't ask questions when it might not be safe to know the answer.

ſixteen

Lorena

By the following season Galaxy had regained its panache. The New York showroom lost part of its luster with Adrienne gone but David was spending a great deal of time there doing considerable vertical and horizontal research to find an appropriate replacement.

He finally settled on a long-legged model-turned-seller name Stephanie Glaser. Steffi, ash blonde, blue eyes and a perpetual tan. Steffi, who had modeled for Ralph Lauren and Versace and knew her way around a showroom...Steffi, with a Texas-bred accent, knew how to party. She fit right in.

Harvey Thompson had sent a lovely spray of flowers to the Temple for Roger's funeral but beyond that there had been no further contact. Will Duval had been replaced as Chief Operating Officer of California Cooking and Starlet Fashions. His current whereabouts were unknown and Charlie was happy to leave it that way.

Roger's funeral had been emotionally difficult. Nearly two hundred people came to Mt. Sinai to pay their respects. Ruby's anger had subsided but the tenuous relationship she and Charlie had been building was ruptured once again.

.

"Daddy," his grown daughter, Katie, had told him when the service was over and the group was moving slowly to the graveside. "Roger had been snorting coke for nearly two years. He'd gotten into a bad group at college and doing marijuana was no longer hip enough for them. I guess I should have told you and Mom at some point but it isn't easy

to snitch on your brother."

"How about you?" Charlie asked. "Do you do drugs also?"

"No way.   Remember, I've been running half-marathons...impossible to do when you're a stoner."

"Thanks for telling me but don't mention it to your mother. Whatever memories she has of Roger should be positive."

"But she blames you. She thinks that all of Roger's bad behavior began in New York."

"She'd blame me even if it began at college. She needs someone to blame for our loss and I'm a good candidate."

Katie kissed her father on the cheek and they walked arm-in-arm up the hill to where Roger would be laid to rest.

Charlie returned to work but found it difficult to get his drive back. He'd just sit in his office staring at pictures of him and Ruby when their children were younger. There was Roger standing next to him...so much promise. It isn't normal to be forced to bury one's child. It should be the other way around the way nature intended.

"You need a new adventure, Charlie," Bunny said. "C'mon, let's go to Disneyland, get away for a day."

"You're kidding, right?" he smiled wanly. "He was such a great kid."

Bunny nodded. There was nothing she could say that would ease her friend's pain.

"He was. But you need to put your loss into one corner of your heart and allow yourself to move forward. Would you like to look at the new Junior line for spring? It looks pretty good."

"If you designed it, I'm sure it's good," he said, trying hard to compose himself.

"Actually, I only oversaw it. I promoted from within and this new girl did me proud."

"Fine, bring it on."

A young Latina girl, her arms full and pushing a rack, scooted in Charlie's office, looking flustered.

"Charlie, this is Lorena Gonzalez...Lorena, Mr. Barron."

"Hi Lorena! Forget the Mister...you call me Charlie and I'll call you Lorena."

"Hi Charlie!"

It wasn't the chimes from Westminster Abbey but their brief exchange caused a perceptible change in the room.

Lorena Gonzalez, an East Los Angeles girl in her early 20's, dark-hair, dark eyes, average height, exuded a charm and innocence with a beautiful face that almost seemed angelic. Charlie stared and Bunny began to feel uncomfortable being there with the two of them.

"Can we look at the line when you're through staring?" she said to Charlie.

Charlie noticed Lorena blushing and he smiled, throwing his hands up in a 'what can I say' manner that even made Bunny laugh. It might be a while before the old Charlie was back, she thought, but at least he's off the ground and moving.

Lorena went through each group, deftly explaining the fabrics, the trim she'd used to embellish each design and the color palette. Charlie was impressed. This girl was thorough and knew her craft. He began to have a renewed zest for the business he'd spent more than thirty years in, and even more important, this girl was dynamite.

When she was finished she gathered up the clothes and began to leave as Charlie picked up one of the tops she'd dropped. They looked at one another briefly as he handed it to her and again, like two teenagers, they both blushed.

"Alright kids, break it up...back to your respective corners," Bunny laughed, shaking her head. "Nice to have you back, Charlie," she said as she left his office.

That afternoon Charlie took one of his frequent walks around the building. It was what he'd always called

MBWA...Management by Walking Around.   This time, however, he made it a point to visit the design room.

More than a dozen women were pinning, sewing, and cutting in an organized frenzy.   Lorena had one blouse draped over her shoulder and pins in her mouth as she huddled over one of the fit models.

"More room for the arm to move...and let the sleeve puff a little here," she said mumbling around the pins.   When she saw Charlie staring at her, the pins all dropped to the floor.

"Mr. Barron, welcome to our little harem," she joked.

"At least there are no eunuchs standing guard."

"No, we have to defend ourselves, but we're a hardy bunch."   It was clear she had become comfortable with the repartee he seemed to enjoy.

"Will you have dinner with me Saturday?"

"Not a good idea.   I like this job and dinner sets us on a dangerous course."

"Nothing like a little danger to add zest to life," he teased.   "I'll pick you up at 7:00."

"How do you know where I live?"

"I looked at your personnel file.   Forgive me, but I needed to make certain you were at least eighteen."

"By more than a few years, I'm afraid."

"Me, too," Charlie laughed and realized that he hadn't laughed much since Roger's death.

He drove to a small home in Canoga Park to pick up Lorena. The house and yard were well-tended...a family proud of where they lived. He wasn't sure his Porsche belonged in the neighborhood as he noticed several teenagers up the street eyeing the sleek silver coupe.

"Good evening, Rodrigo," he said, a little uncomfortably. Lorena's father had opened the door on its first knock. He had seen his Fabric Manager only yesterday at work and this new relationship was a strain for them both.

"Señor Barron, welcome to my home. This is my wife, Lupe."

Lupe nodded and smiled cautiously. She wanted to see this important man who employed both her husband and her daughter. The three of them stood, not sure what small talk could ease the tension. Only a few minutes passed silently but it felt much longer.

"You look lovely, Lorena. Your parents and I were just chatting," he lied.

"Thank you, Charlie. We can go. Adiós Mama...Papa."

"Did you enjoy your 'chat'?" she said in a mocking tone.

"Actually, I froze. It was embarrassing seeing your father at work and now being in his home dating his daughter."

"Imagine how difficult it was for him."

"I made us a reservation at a place north of Malibu I haven't been to in years."

"Anywhere is fine," she said, rolling down the window and letting the wind blow through her hair, music from the car's stereo system filling her senses.

Charlie hadn't been back to Toscana in years but Signor Signorelli remembered him as if it was last week.

"Signore Charlie, it has been much too long but you have not aged."

"You continue to lie beautifully. This is my friend, Lorena Gonzalez."

He greeted her warmly, and understood immediately that Mrs. Barron, Ruby, was no longer Charlie's woman. He lit a candle on their table and brought them a carafe of his best Chianti. The restaurant was still half-empty but neither he nor his guests seemed to mind.

It was a pleasant evening. The couple chatted and they laughed...a relaxed, no-pressure laugh. Before midnight Charlie pulled his car to a stop in front of Lorena's home.

"Thank you, Charlie," Lorena said, leaning over, putting her hand on his cheek and kissing him lightly. Charlie could feel the heat rising in his groin and tried to will it to disappear.

"How about next Saturday? Oops, it will have to be the following week. I need to fly to San Francisco...unless you'd like to go with me?"

"Really? I love San Francisco. Are you sure?"

"Absolutely. And…to be on the safe side, explain to your parents we'll have separate rooms at the Fairmont."

"Goodnight, Charlie. You've been a perfect gentleman."

"For Christ's sakes, Charlie, don't you ever learn?" Bunny said. "You took that young designer to The Limited a few years ago and came back with a large order and the crabs. Now you want to take a different young designer to San Francisco. You are definitely the most perpetually horny man I've ever known."

"Ah, yes….Tammy King! I remember! A gymnastics wonder," he laughed. "I wonder whatever happened to her."

"She's probably fat with her tits hanging to her waist and three ugly kids."

"Ooh, that's a visual I don't want to dwell on."

"So what about Lorena? Please find someone else to dawdle with."

"I'm not dawdling…we just have fun together."

"You're going to hurt her and I'm going to get royally pissed. I like her and she's a good designer."

"I hear you. Now get the fuck out of my office. I have work to do."

"Fine, close the door and masturbate…then let her know she's not going away with you for the weekend."

It was a windy day as Charlie and Lorena bicycled across the Golden Gate Bridge. She was enjoying herself. He was wondering what the hell he was doing on two wheels struggling to keep his balance.

"This would be a problem for me on a calm day," he shouted ten feet ahead to a disappearing figure.

"Almost there," she said as she turned her head.

They stopped at the far end of the bridge, just above Sausalito, the San Francisco skyline outlined across the water, Coit Tower and the Transamerica building pasted against a cloudless sky. She was laughing as she came up to Charlie straddling his bike, clearly out of breath.

She kissed him chastely as he let the bicycle fall and took her in his arms, held her head up to him and looked into her eyes. A few moments later Charlie hailed a cab and threw the bikes inside.

"Fairmont Hotel!

It was noon before they emerged from Lorena's room. Charlie returned to his own room long enough for each of them to shower, dress, and take a cable car to Fisherman's Wharf. He was enjoying playing tourist.

By the time they took their flight back to Los Angeles Sunday evening they were more than just friends.

"Charlie, is this really what you want?" Lorena asked as the plane taxied down the runway.

"To have a good time? Sure. Isn't that what everyone wants? We've had a wonderful weekend and with luck we'll have many more."

"I'm grateful, Charlie. I really enjoy being with you but just having a good time isn't enough for me. I want something more from life."

"Lorena, you are so young. You'll find your Lochinvar...your Prince Charming, and settle down to the American dream...2 ½ kids and a dog, but in the meantime enjoy the good times."

He took her to her door, kissed her and smiled. "See you at work...don't be late...the boss will be pissed."

"What the hell did you do to Lorena?" Bunny asked the middle of the following week. "She works...she cries...she shouts at the sewers. She never did those things before."

"What are you blaming me for? We had a terrific time in San Francisco. Now we're back at work."

"You actually have no idea, do you?"

"What? I don't know what you're talking about. Say, did you see David's new car? A Lamborghini...yellow. The cops are going to see it coming for miles...they won't need radar."

"Charlie, I was talking about Lorena...the young girl you obviously seduced last weekend."

"Bunny, the girl is a grown woman...give her some credit."

"I give her lots of credit but not a lot of points for good judgment or she wouldn't have gone with you."

Lorena waited until most everyone had gone home before walking softly into Charlie's office. Several weeks had elapsed since their San Francisco trip. Charlie had stopped calling but, she rationalized, he was traveling a lot.

"Charlie, got a minute?" She said, peeking into his office.

"Sure...c'mon on in? Want something to drink?"

"No, I just wanted to know if something was wrong. I haven't heard from you."

"Just chaotic...work...traveling. I even spent a weekend with my daughter."

"I'm pregnant," Lorena blurted out, dropping into a chair, crying, her secret finally shared.

"Oh, that is a problem," Charlie said, walking over to her, pulling up a chair and taking her hand.

"Lorena, this can be handled. I like you...I really do but I don't think I'm ready to be a father again and settle down. We'll find somewhere you can go where they handle these sorts of things very discreetly."

"Charlie, I'm Catholic. We don't handle these sorts of things. I'm going to have your child."

"Lorena, this is the '80's and you are an intelligent woman. You have options. If that's the path you choose, so be it. I disagree...that's all I can do."

"Puta!" He said the profane word with an anger and vitriol that emanated from deep within his very soul. He knew the word would sting...he wanted it to hurt her. He loved his daughter so much...he had expected so much from her and now, the ultimate failure... she was pregnant.

"Don't say that," his wife shouted. "She is not a puta!"

"She spreads her legs for a man she isn't married to...a man old enough to be her father. That is what a puta does," he responded, his voice cracking with emotion.

"Daddy, I'm so sorry," Lorena Gonzalez cried, tears staining her bronze cheeks. "He said he loved me and I loved him. I've been such a fool. When I told him I was pregnant, he just smiled and offered to pay for an abortion. I explained I was Catholic and that wasn't an option. He just shrugged and walked away, muttering 'your choice.' "

Rodrigo's choice was that Lorena go to Mexico and stay with her grandmother until the baby was born. After watching his daughter board the Mexicana DC-3 for her flight to Monterrey, and drying his wife's tears, he drove to the factory. He walked into the front offices of Galaxy, past the Koi pond and the white Macaw that were Barron's treasures, past Barron's secretary, and into the large office that housed the company's owner.

"You can't go in there," Judy Kaffer shouted, rising from behind her desk and trying, unsuccessfully, to block the way.

Barron stood as his Fabric Manager stormed into his office. He knew Rodrigo as a gentle man, hard-working, and a man who kept impeccable records of yards, dye lots, and end cuts. Charlie also knew that Lorena was Rodrigo's daughter.

"Rodrigo, I'm glad you're here. I'd….." Charlie's words were cut short by a right fist smashing against his left cheek and into his nose. The blow drove the larger man to the floor, blood spurting everywhere. Judy and several others watched from the door, inert, startled by the suddenness of the event.

"Someone call the police!" Judy reacted as Rodrigo walked past her with the same purposeful stride that had carried him into Barron's office.

"No," Barron shouted. "Fuck him! Let him go."

Bunny hired a replacement for Lorena and Charlie replaced Rodrigo, but the chemistry within Galaxy had changed. Bunny avoided Charlie as much as she could and both Papa and Lili, his Shipping and Production Managers, shunned him.

The three of them were chatting around Papa's desk in the shipping area a month after Lorena was gone.

"I think I'm going to resign," Lili said. "I always liked Charlie until now, but this thing he's doing is shitty and it's hard to respect him. I don't do well working for someone I can't respect."

"I don't know why," Papa said. He'd always made it a point to keep his opinions to himself. "…But Charlie's pecker has always dictated his actions."

"For sure," Bunny added, "And I've known him a long time. We could all quit."

"Let's throw a big party for her and the baby when they return from Mexico. I'm still in contact with Rodrigo. He'll let me know," Papa said.

Charlie felt the chill. Even when he went to Baroness's on Montana, there was a difference. And it wasn't as if he was immune to missing Lorena. As long as she worked in the Design room, it was fine, but as soon as she left he began missing her smile and her laughter, even when they just passed one another. In truth she was too young for him. He should never have taken her to San Francisco and gotten so involved. What the fuck was he thinking?

They held the party at Margarita Jones, a popular Mexican restaurant on Figueroa. Even Judy, Charlie's Secretary, had decided that everyone would just take an extended lunch. Margaritas flowed by the pitcher while everyone ogled the new baby boy.

Despite vocal objections from her parents, Lorena had named the boy Roger. And there was no question this was Charlie's son. He had dark wavy hair and penetrating brown eyes. And he smiled...he loved to gurgle and have people fuss over him. It seemed he was enjoying the party as much as the other guests.

Lorena found it difficult to fight back her tears at all the wonderful well-wishers and the things they'd brought for the baby. She hadn't realized she had so many friends.

Back at Galaxy David walked past all the unanswered phones and into Charlie's office.

"Are they all still at the party for Lorena?" he asked, sadly, and pouring himself a drink.

"Yes," David responded. "I stayed for a little while but then begged off. You need to go there, Charlie. Your absence is upsetting everyone in the company."

"It would be worse if I were there."

"Did you know she named the baby 'Roger'?"

"Shit! Why the fuck did she do that? Ruby will go ballistic."

"He looks like you."

"Pity the poor kid."

David walked out leaving Charlie to his own thoughts. A few minutes later David watched as Charlie left the building. He hoped it was to do something right.

Charlie sat in his car at the far end of the Margarita Jones parking lot. It was nearly three, late for the lunch crowd, too early for dinner. He waited until most of his employees had left. Finally, he crossed the lot and found where the party had been held.

There were three women sitting, looking over the array of gifts and cards. Lorena, her mother, and Bunny were sitting together. He realized how beautiful Lorena was. Bunny was holding the baby. The women stopped talking the moment they saw Charlie staring at them.

Bunny stood and handed the baby boy to Charlie.

"Meet your son," she said.   Then she took Lorena's mother and left the room.

Charlie stared at the baby. This was his son. He walked over to Lorena and sat down. There were tears in her eyes.

"I've missed you, Charlie. All those months in Monterrey I thought what I would say if we saw one another again and now I can't remember any of them."

"He's beautiful, Lorena. He has your eyes and coloring."

"That's the Mexican in him. The hair and his features are all you."

"You know you shouldn't have named him Roger but…" he paused. "I think I'm glad you did. He reminds me of my Roger the first time I saw him at the hospital."

"What are we going to do, Charlie? I want you in our lives. We both need you."

"You know I'm here for you and the baby. I'm happy to provide whatever is necessary."

"You're what's necessary," she said.

"I don't know if I can make that commitment. I'd be a terrible husband. I'm too old. I'd philander every chance I had. You don't need that."

"You're right but I'm stuck loving you."

"You know your father really belted me," Charlie laughed.

"He hasn't been too pleased with me either," she admitted.

"Let's take it slow," he said. "Can we do that?"

Lorena nodded and the three of them walked out into the late afternoon sun.

Three months later Miss Lorena Gonzalez and Mr. Charles Barron were married. In attendance were all the employees of Galaxy Fashions and a few hundred other close friends. Highlight of the ceremony was baby Roger Barron, acting as Ring Bearer, gripping the ring in his tiny fingers and being carried by Miss Katie Barron. Mr. and Mrs. Rodrigo Gonzalez cried tears of happiness.

And, in the last row, wearing large sun glasses and a sweater over her blue sari, sat Jessica, holding a small brown dog, Coco II.

Charlie never did stop straying but he always came home to Lorena and what would eventually be another son and daughter.

Author's Note

In the 1960's, all the way through the 1980's, the apparel industry in the United States thrived. Nearly 800,000 people across the country were engaged in the design, production, and sales of children's, men's, and women's apparel...and almost everything was manufactured in this country.

There were a plethora of retailers to sell to and the financial resources needed to start a new company was relatively small. Men like Charlie Barron dominated the scene in New York and Los Angeles. Illegal aliens from Mexico and Central America poured into the country and the sweatshops of sewing contractors. The lure of jobs made the flow impossible to stop. Everyone wanted to look good and Charlie and his brethren provided a steady stream of product to large retailers who were opening more and more stores in malls across suburbia.

Then a series of changes took place that had a profound effect. The garments that had always been sewn in California and New York, had already moved to cheaper labor hubs, such as Tennessee. Then NAFTA, the North American Free Trade Act, made it cheaper to produce garments in Mexico. A few years later China was granted full entry into the WTO, World Trade Organization. Suddenly, the availability of cheap cotton and cheaper labor moved American companies to produce off-shore.

At the other end the emergence of discounters and box-stores, such as Walmart, Costco, and Target, gave them the leverage to produce their own goods. Sear's was forced to merge with K-Mart, and both continue to struggle. Mergers reduced the number of retailers. Today, domestic apparel manufacturing employment is closer to 200,000...25% of its peak.

But during that post World War II hey-day there was an excitement, a time of good guys and bad guys, a time of sex, drugs, and fashion.

Acknowledgements

My deepest gratitude goes to those who helped by reading, suggesting, and correcting my manuscript, my tendency to overuse the past pluperfect tense, and a forgetfulness at inserting commas. Linda Martin, Lauren Silinsky, and Arleen Tisherman have all been wonderful in giving their time and encouragement. Greg Marquette was most helpful in recommending changes to the story and long-time friends in the industry contributed some delightful anecdotes. Jon Jackson, as always, has been there to help with my computer frustrations and his publishing support. Arlene Matza-Jackson came up with the idea for the cover and James Kirtley executed it beautifully. My thanks to each of you.

About the Author

Carole Eglash-Kosoff lives and writes in Valley Village, California. She graduated from UCLA and spent her career teaching, writing, and traveling to more than seventy countries. She was Controller and Chief Financial  Officer of several apparel companies and owner of the only button manufacturing plant in the Western United States.

In 2006, following the death of her husband, mother, and brother within a month, she spent several months teaching in the black townships of South Africa. Her first book, **The Human Spirit – Apartheid's Unheralded Heroes,** tells the true life stories of an amazing array of men and women who have devoted their lives during the worst years of apartheid to help the children, the elderly, and the disabled of the townships. These people cared when no one else did and their efforts continue to this day. This book has also been presented as a stage play.

An avid student of history, she researched the decades preceding and following the Civil War for nearly two years, including time in Louisiana, the setting for **Winds of Change** and her earlier novel, **When Stars Align.**

When Stars Align, was a well-received novel of mixed race lovers, Thaddeus, colored, born from the rape of a young slave girl by the scion of the plantation, Moss Grove. His love for Amy, white, carries them both through the Civil War and Reconstruction but their stars never align. It is also currently under consideration as a 3-part mini-series.

Winds of Change, released in late 2011, follows the characters of **When Stars Align** into the decades that closed out one century and led us into the next, decades that saw the introduction of the automobile, the airplane, and the telephone as well as the Spanish-American War, and World War I. They are both stories of mixed race love during a period of terrible injustice. They are stories of war, reconstruction, and racism, but most of all; they are stories of hope.

BY ONE VOTE is her 4th book. It tells twelve true stories of significant events in America's history resolved by a single vote. The concept of this book had been with her for several decades but it would take the evolution of the internet and her love of history to complete the research necessary.

Learn more about other books:

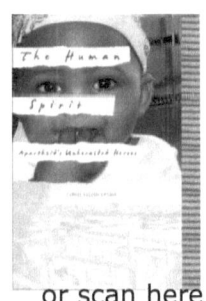

The Human Spirit
– Apartheid's Unheralded Heroes

ISBN #978-1-4520-3306-8 (Softback)

More information is available on the
website: www.thehumanspirit-thebook.com

or scan here

Prologue

Apartheid in South Africa has now been gone more than fifteen years but the heroes of their struggle to achieve a Black majority-run democracy are still being revealed. Some individuals toiled publicly, but most worked tirelessly in the shadows to improve the welfare of the Black and Colored populations that had been so neglected. Nelson Mandela was still in prison; clean water and sanitation barely existed; AIDS was beginning to orphan an entire generation.

Meanwhile a white, Jewish, middle class woman, joined with Tutu, Millie, Ivy, Zora and other concerned Black women, respectfully called Mamas, to help those most in need, often being beaten and arrested by white security police.

This book tells the story of these women and others who have spent their adult lives making South Africa a better place for those who were the country's most disadvantaged.

When Stars Align

ISBN#978-1-4567-3890-7 (Softback)

More information is available on the website:

www.whenstarsalign-thebook.com

or **scan here**

Prologue

The love that Thaddeus and Amy feel for one another can get them both killed. He is colored, an ex-slave, and she is white. In 19th century Louisiana mixed race relationships are both illegal and unacceptable.

Moss Grove, a large Mississippi River cotton plantation has thrived from the use of slave labor while its owners lived lives of comfort and privilege. Thaddeus, born more than a decade earlier from the rape of a young field slave by the heir to the plantation, is raised as a Moss Grove house servant. His presence remains a thorn in the side of the man who sired him.

Deepening divisiveness between North and South launches the Civil War and changes Moss Grove in ways no one could have anticipated. With the war swirling we see the battles and carnage through Thaddeus' eyes. The war ends and he returns to Moss Grove and to Amy, hoping to enjoy their newly won freedoms. With the help of Union soldiers, schools are established to educate those who were formerly prohibited from learning to read. Medical clinics are opened and businesses begun. Black legislators are elected and help to pass new laws. Hope flourishes. Perhaps the stars will now finally align for the young lovers.

In 1876, however, the ex-Confederate states barter the selection of President Rutherford B. Hayes for removal of all Union troops from their soil in the most contested election in American history. Within a decade hopes are dashed as Jim Crow laws are passed, the Ku Klux Klan launches new violence, and black progress is crushed.

'When Stars Align' is a soaring novel of memorable white, Negro, and colored men and women set against actual historic events.

****

Winds Of Change

ISBN#978-0-9839601-0-2 (Softback)
ISBN#978-0-9839601-1-9 (eBook)

More information is available on the website:
www.windsofchange-thebook.com

or scan here

Prologue

The racially charged love and conflict of the critically acclaimed ***When Stars Align*** become more entrenched after the Civil War and Reconstruction. Amy had taken her daughter, nephew, and a son she'd had never been able to acknowledge, born from her love with Thaddeus, her colored lover, to San Francisco, as a refuge from the intense racial scrutiny of the South.

They are forced to return to their old home, Moss Grove, a successful Mississippi River cotton plantation, as young adults. They discover facts about themselves that refute everything they believed regarding both their parents and their racial background. It changes the lives of each of them. Bess and Stephen's love is thwarted. Josiah struggles with echoes of his past.

It is a tumultuous time in American history that includes the inventions of airplanes, automobiles, telephones and movies midst decades of lynching's and economic turmoil. It is the Spanish-American War and World War I. Racial biases complicate lives and relationships as newly arrived immigrants vie with white and Negro workers all trying to gain a piece of the American dream. **Winds of Change** is a soaring historic fiction novel that stands alone but follows the next generation from those we came to know in **When Stars Align** into the 20th century. It is a socially relevant, historically accurate, saga of decades often overlooked in American history.

****

By One Vote

ISBN#978-0-9839601-2-6
Published by Valley Village Publishing 2012
www.byonevote-thebook.com

We live in a period of economic and political unrest and we believe it to be worse than at any time in our history...but it isn't. America's two hundred plus years of existence has been one of turmoil, dissension, and war. It has been a time of economic growth and stagnation. Each decade has found

stalwarts and dissenters convinced that they, alone, have the best solution for the country's ills.

A surprising number of events that altered the country's direction resulted from the vote of a single individual either in support of a change or opposed to it. Names such as James Bayard, Edmund Ross, and Joseph Bradley are unknown but they altered the fabric or our nation as significantly as more famous Americans. This book, *By One Vote*, tells these stories. The events are factual, the dramatizations surrounding them are the studied imagination of the author.

View a summary of the book on You Tube:
http://youtu.be/tIDBJc7JUEQ

www.ingramcontent.com/pod-product-compliance
Lightning Source LLC
Chambersburg PA
CBHW030426180626
46812CB00005B/2206